THE
RE-MIX

XANDRA PHILLIPS

Two Shoes Publishing House
The Re-Mix
Copyright © 2011 by Xandra Phillips

ISBN – 978-09842933-7-7

9 7 8 0 9 8 4 2 9 3 3 7 7

Cover art: Created by Artisticco© – License purchased at dreamstime.com

Dear Reader,

Welcome to The Re-Mix There are a lot of characters in this book, so I want to give you a quick overview. I'm almost sure it won't be a problem, because you probably already know these people. They are the friends you grew up with, and years later you'd still do anything for them.

Malcolm is the reformed party boy. He was a mess in his younger days, but eventually got himself together and is now very successful.

Imani is your loud-mouthed girlfriend. She doesn't hold her tongue for anyone or anything. There is never any doubt about what she's thinking because she always tells it all.

Quentin is the all-American guy. He's the great guy that everyone loves. He's handsome, funny and smart.

Raegan is the planner. She has a plan for everything, especially her life. When plan "A" doesn't turn out the way she expects, she has plan "B" ready.

Garrison a.k.a. "G" is the comedian of the group. He always has a smart remark ready. Even if he doesn't say it, you see it in his eyes.

Stacia is the one who was voted most likely to succeed. She's gorgeous, smart and ambitious.

Trent was also a party boy, but where Malcolm was out to get the ladies, Trent was happy to party all night for the sake of partying. He also got himself together and turned out to be very successful.

Morgana was a head-turner back in the day, and she still is. She got involved in the church as she got older but remained "cool".

Keith was your boy, back in the day. He was the one that you went to with all your problems. He was no angel, but matured nicely and ended up becoming a minister.

Abril is the strong single mom who has to keep everything together. She got pregnant when she was young but managed to come out on top.

I know it seems like a lot, but like I said, you probably know people like them. You may even be one of them. The point is, don't get caught up in the number of names. Just sit back and enjoy the book. Ultimately it's a story about friendship and how it makes our lives better.

DEDICATION

I've heard it said that friends are the family you get to choose. I'd like to dedicate this book to my friends. My life is better because of you.

Chapter 1

"Who's your daddy? Come on, baby. Say it. Who's your daddy?"

The damp, handsome face was contorted with pleasure as he leaned over the writhing body beneath him.

"Come on, baby! Baby!"

"Arrghhh!" Jade woke up in a sweat and breathing hard.

"What is wrong with you?" Callie, her college roommate, poked her head into the small room a moment later. They had been lucky to get this suite in their junior year. It was usually reserved for seniors at the prestigious university.

Jade moved the limp lock of hair out of her eyes. "If I have one more sex dream, I swear, I'll…"

Callie laughed. "You'll what? Go find your boo?"

"No. He's not my boo. Not anymore."

"Good. Even though he was yummy. You don't need the headache."

Jade nodded. "I know. I've got enough to do without worrying about that idiot."

"Amen to that girl. Any guy that would sleep around with six different women at the same time needs to be strung up. By the way, your mom called this morning."

"Oh, okay, thanks. I'll call her sometime this weekend. I need to get through this Art History exam first. I still have to finish going over the section on The Harlem Renaissance."

Callie smiled. "I absolutely love The Harlem Renaissance."

Jade was nowhere near excited. "What's so special about it?"

Callie looked at Jade like she'd lost her mind. "Are you kidding me? Besides the fact that it produced some of the most incredible pieces of art, music, and literature that the world has ever seen, it was kismet."

Jade sat up. "I get the whole art thing. That's why I'm taking the class. But what do you mean by kismet?"

Callie's hands started gesturing wildly. "It was like all the planets aligned and God smiled down on the earth just at the right time to bring all the right people together. Think about it. If all of them hadn't made it to that exact spot at that exact same time, it wouldn't have worked. Everyone had to be there to contribute to the rebirth and reawakening. It was fate."

"Hmm." Jade nodded. "You always have the best insight." She was sure Callie was going to be in charge of something very important one day.

"Aw, thanks, but get to studying. And don't forget to call your mom."

***

"How are the plans coming for your reunion?"

Stacia looked across the desk at her handsome client. He really was beautiful, much prettier than her, and she was no slouch. "Good, actually. I spoke to my girls yesterday and everyone will be there. You should come with me."

Richard looked dubious. "Come with you? Why would I do that? I didn't even finish college."

"You turned out fine, even without a college degree. Besides, Atlanta is full of people looking to buy what you're selling. We can set up a PR event the day before my reunion and you can put your pretty face in front of plenty of cameras. It's a good opportunity to meet some perspective clients."

"Well, that's true. But that flight across country is so ridiculously long."

"Oh, quit your whining. It's only a few hours and I'll put you up in my suite so you won't have a hotel expense."

"It's a few hours and a major time change. It takes all day to get out there."

Stacia sighed. Richard could be such a diva. "It will only be for a few days. We'll leave out of Vegas on Thursday, set up the event for Friday, do the reunion stuff on Saturday and we'll be out by Sunday morning."

"I don't know." Richard still looked doubtful.

She flashed her most disarming smile. "Come on, Richard, do it for your favorite marketing exec? You know, the one that cuts you a break on every single deal we've ever made."

"Fine, I'll go, I can always use more clients and business is business."

"That's all I'm saying."

Richard left her office about thirty minutes later. The door hadn't been closed for a second before Stacia pulled out her smart phone. The instant message was still front and center on her phone's glass screen. It was this text message that popped up earlier that moved her into action.

BTW, QUENTIN SAID HE WAS COMING TOO.

It was from her girlfriend, Imani, who apparently stayed in contact with all the friends from the old group. Stacia kept in touch with all of the girls and most of the guys, but she hadn't brought herself to the point where she could talk to **him** yet.

It was absurd, she knew, especially since it had been over twenty years since the break-up, but she couldn't help it. She couldn't walk into the reunion alone, knowing he would show up with someone else. Stacia tried hard, but she couldn't remember why they had broken up in the first place. It doesn't take much for teenagers, though. You break up on a whim when you think there are a million people you could possibly hook up with.

Twenty-something years later she knew better. You only find the person who you click with on every level once in a lifetime, twice if you're lucky. Quentin was that person for her. He was gorgeous and smart with a wicked sense of humor, and for some reason that she couldn't remember she let him go.

She may not remember why they broke up, but she remembered clear as day when he walked into the homecoming tent during their junior year with Julia Ronson. He knew she would be there. She had been volunteering to register alumni for the event when she saw them. He purposely walked around the whole tent with Julia on his arm, and still managed to avoid eye contact with Stacia. She'd felt so completely and utterly humiliated. She made sure to steer clear of him after that. It wasn't easy, but for the next year and a half she managed to evade him. They didn't even speak at graduation, and that was the last time she'd seen him. That was the reason she hadn't seen him in over twenty years.

Stacia shut her laptop down before locking up her office for the night. Humiliation was a hard pill to swallow and if she could help it, it wouldn't be happening again, at least not to her. Richard's confirmation just made sure of that.

***

Imani hung up the phone with Raegan in anticipation. She hadn't been with all her girls in a long time, five years to be exact. She hadn't seen them in the same room since the last reunion. She looked around her nice suburban home outside Birmingham and conjured up thoughts of the last time they were together. They had met at a restaurant right after the last reunion and ended up talking all night. Management finally asked them to leave at two that morning.

She missed them so much. Now that they were older, she felt better knowing she would see them again soon. So many people were dying at a young

10

age. She just needed to make sure every one was fine.

These class reunions were so you could see your friends, sure, but in her mind they were also a check-in of sorts. She hated the part of the reunion when they read the names of those who were no longer with us. Life was way too short and hers was way too empty. She needed to know that there was more to life than her job, and her girlfriends helped her see that. They talked often enough but it wasn't the same as being with them. She was much better when she could see and touch the people she was talking to.

Yes, she had a big mouth, but anyone who knew her knew she was a softie at heart. And nothing did her heart better than to get together with real friends. Friends that knew you and still stuck around were the best kind. And these friends she was about to reconnect with were the best. She only had two more weeks to wait.

***

Raegan rolled over and looked at Trent as he snored quietly. Who'd have thought they would have ever hooked up? It certainly would not have been her. They were friends all through college, but she was no closer to him than the rest of the group. Then her company moved her down to Dallas from Phoenix and it was like starting all over again. She had to learn a new city and make new friends. It was only natural that she'd turn to Trent, one of her oldest friends to help her get acclimated.

He helped her all right. A house warming party here, a mojito there and next thing you know, they were together. It didn't occur overnight, but since they'd gotten to know each other long ago, the foundation of friendship was already firmly established. There was nothing new to learn about him. She knew it all and she was comfortable with it. He must've felt the same way because two weeks ago, he invited her to his place for dinner. After a night of passionate lovemaking, he cooked her breakfast the next morning. They'd been inseparable ever since.

He had been divorced for almost fifteen years, marrying right out of college. "Wrong move," in his own words. Raegan's dead body was a little fresher. Her divorce had been finalized a little over two years ago. She swore to herself that it would be her first and last marriage. Her ex- was a nice guy, made decent money and actually remembered her birthday for most of the time they had been together, but they had nothing in common. She knew it when he proposed, knew it and said yes anyway. She especially felt it when she walked down the aisle seven years ago.

Looking back, the best thing she could remember about her wedding day was the night before. All her girlfriends had flown out and thrown her the bachelorette party of the century. Those were the days. Now here she was doing something she swore she'd never do again. Actually, she really couldn't say "again" because she hadn't really been in love with her husband. Marrying him had been more of a practical move. She was in her mid-thirties at the time and alone. She didn't want to die without ever having had a husband, so she just jumped in.

It was nice for what it was, but after the newness wore off, it was just there. It wasn't good or bad, exciting or dull. It was just a marriage to a guy she looked at more like a brother than anything else. So when he popped up a few years later and said he was having an affair with an old girlfriend, she was happy for him. Who was she to stand in the way of true love or lust or whatever he thought it was. Truth be told, she was happy to get out.

She had started to think that true love wasn't for her. After all, not everybody finds their soul mate. She was forty when the ink on the divorce decree dried and she swore to herself that day that she wouldn't get involved in another relationship, not seriously anyway. She was too old for that.

But forever is a long time and here she was, falling in love with one of her best friends and wondering if he felt the same way. She didn't even tell Morgana about the relationship and she told Morgana almost everything. She couldn't help it. It was like the girl had some special power to draw the deepest, darkest secrets out of people. She wondered what Morgana or the rest of their friends would think about this new relationship. Not that she planned to tell them. She wanted to keep this just between her and Trent for the moment. Eventually, though, they would have to be told and when they were told, she wondered how they would take it.

Oh well, que sera, sera.

***

"Sister Morgana, can I talk to you for a second?"

Morgana spun around and eyed the dowdy young woman quickly. She was on her way out of the church and really wanted to get home but she could spare a few extra minutes. It was church after all.

"Sure, Diana. What is it?"

"I just want to know, how do you have all the guys in church chasing you down and the rest of us can't get a glance?"

Morgana chose her words carefully in order not to offend the young woman.

"Before I answer that Diana, can I ask you a personal question?"

The girl looked nervous. "Yes."

"Is there some reason you always wear skirts down to your ankles and no makeup?"

"Well, my grandmother always said makeup and short skirts were the devil's work."

Just then, one of the church members walked by.

"Goodnight ladies."

Morgana waved. "Goodnight David." She noticed that Diana hadn't moved. Morgana smiled. "He's handsome." Diana simply looked down.

"Diana, it's simple. If you want to attract guys, you need to put your best foot forward. No one said you had to come into church looking like a streetwalker. Moderate makeup and appropriate length skirts will go a long way in getting you where you want to be."

"I just, I mean I don't know how to…"

"What are you doing tomorrow?"

"Nothing."

Morgana hooked arms with the young girl and ushered her toward the door.

"I need to talk to my girlfriend, Abril in the morning, but after that I'll be shopping and going to get my hair done. Would you like to join me?"

"Yes!" Diana's face displayed the excitement of a child.

"Good. Bring whatever extra shopping money you have. You'll look like a new woman by Sunday."

Morgana hugged her new protégé as they said goodbye in the parking lot. She really couldn't blame the young woman, not when she had someone on her mind as well. She had run into Keith last week at a church function in downtown Atlanta where she and her church members were the guests of another ministry. She was shocked when she saw him sitting in the pulpit. He was part of the group of friends she'd hung out with all through college. She had known him for over twenty years but they only ever looked at each other as friends. They'd kept in touch here and there, but last week when they saw each other, something was different. There was an extra spark or something going on. Morgana didn't know what it was, but she was willing to explore it at the reunion. She would be looking for eye catching outfits this weekend just as much as Diana.

***

"Abril? Good, I caught you. I'm so sorry, dear, but I need to change our cabin preference again."

"No problem, Mrs. Handley. We're on central time here in Denver so we're an hour behind you all. I've got plenty of time before I shut my system down yet. So, you want to go from an inside suite to an outside suite?"

"That's right dear."

"Okay, and would you like a balcony or no balcony?"

"Sweetie, don't entice me. I'm liable to come back a happy widow if there's a balcony attached to our cabin. All that ocean… they'd never find him. No, the temptation would be too great."

Abril's laughter filled her office. "Yes ma'am, no balcony for you. " A few keystrokes later, Abril had handled the request quickly. "All right, you're all set. Your ten day cruise takes off in two weeks."

"Thanks, honey. You're my favorite travel agent. That's why I keep coming back to you. You always have just the right touch. Now how's that little cutie pie of yours, Miss Jade, doing?"

Abril smiled at the mention of her daughter's name. The circumstances that brought her into the world weren't exactly happy, but she was the light of Abril's world. Abril would be the first to admit her bias, but it couldn't be helped. The child was smart, funny and beautiful. The color of her eyes decided her name.

"She's great. She'll be finishing her third year of college in a week."

Mrs. Handley gasped. "College? Oh my goodness. I bet you're planning a big vacation. Seems like she was just starting high school."

Abril nodded. "I know. My baby grew up fast, but she's staying through the summer to take extra courses. She's trying to complete a double major.

I've got a big round-the-world trip planned for her graduation. "

"Oh, that sounds lovely, dear. Give her my love next time you speak with her."

"I sure will, and don't forget to pack the sunscreen this time, Mrs. Handley. We don't want any mishaps like last time."

The older woman's laughter traveled through the speaker on the phone.

"We most certainly do not. Being mistaken for a lobster on a beach is one thing. Having it happen in an ocean full of carnivores is another. Thank you, dear, I won't forget this time. Thanks for all your help, and I'll send pictures to add to the wall once we're back."

"Thank you, and have a great trip."

Abril hung up the phone and spun around to face the wall Mrs. Handley had just mentioned. It was full of smiling vacationers in sunny spots. She started asking everyone she booked on a trip to send her a picture a while ago and over ten years later, the ten by ten wall was nearly filled. She posted the best looking pictures on her website, knowing those smiling faces would help make up the minds of those trying to decide whether or not they should use Isle of Jade Travel Service.

She planned to use the pictures from Jade's graduation trip to fill in any blank spaces. Or, the way business was going, she may have to start another wall. Twenty years ago she didn't know how she was going to make it, but she'd held on and life was good now. In a couple of weeks she would go celebrate twenty years away from college with her friends. She tried to push out of her mind that she would also, inevitably, be seeing Jade's father. But it was only a weekend. She could handle one weekend.

Chapter 2

"All right class of '91, let's show the old timers how it's done. Come on out here and dance, but save some for tonight. We've got a lot planned for you this weekend."

The DJ behind the turntable had the downtown park jumping. The place was crawling with people. Classmates along with their spouses and children ate, laughed, talked and played. The classes ending with a one or a six had staked their claim. And if you weren't part of a reunion class from the historically black college, you quickly figured out that you weren't welcome.

Quentin parked his rental car almost a half-mile from where he could see the balloons and tents set up. He couldn't get any closer if he tried. It looked like the city of Atlanta was filled to capacity. Anticipation built up as he drew closer to the park gates. He hadn't seen most of his friends in five years, not since the last reunion. He hadn't seen Stacia in twenty years. She had conveniently managed to avoid him for that long.

At the five-year reunion, he had to work in a different state on Monday morning and could only come to the reunion on Friday night. She didn't come into town until Saturday morning. At the ten-year reunion, she brought her now ex- husband and he wasn't all that interested in meeting the guy, so he really couldn't blame that one on her. At the fifteen-year reunion, he brought his now ex-wife, and Stacia made herself scare once again.

Well, it had been twenty years and enough was enough. They had unfinished business to settle and Quentin planned to do everything in his power to settle it before he left for Chicago on Sunday morning.

Malcolm looked up to see Quentin standing near the area set up for the class of '86. He set his plate down to mark his spot and headed over to greet his old friend. They talked fairly often, but he hadn't seen Quentin in five years.

"What's up, brother!" Malcolm stuck his hand out and Quentin took hold of it before they clapped each other on the back.

"Mal, man, it's good to see you. What's going on with you?"

"It's all good, bruh. Come on back this way. You're in the section set up for the class of '86. I only got here a few minutes ago, myself. I had to check on my Gran."

Quentin took a look around. "I was wondering why I didn't recognize any of these faces. How's your Granny doing, anyway?"

"She's good, hasn't changed a bit."

Quentin smiled. "I sure miss her cooking. Tell her I said hello next time you see her."

"Will do."

"So are we this way?"

"Yeah, we're on this side of the park." Malcolm pointed and then walked toward the area. "How was your flight in?"

"Hey, any flight where the plane touches down is a good flight in my book."

"I hear you." Malcolm stopped to show Quentin the layout of the reunion area. "Most of the food is in that tent over there, but they've got some in the small tent next to the grill. And the bathroom is that way."

They both turned to look up the hill and whom should they see but Stacia and Richard. She saw them too, but no one spoke. When the moment passed, Malcolm pointed to the table where his food rested. "I'm set up over here." He watched as Quentin's eyes followed Stacia until she was out of sight.

"Q?"

"Hmm?"

"I said I'm over here."

"Right." He walked with Malcolm over to the designated table and took a seat.

"So how's the food?"

Malcolm chased the last of a hotdog with a swig of soda. "It's kind of hard to mess up burgers and dogs man, you should go get a plate. On second thought, Stacia and her pretty boyfriend just went up there. You might wanna hang back."

Quentin looked over at the tent. "Whatever, man. I'm just as pretty as he is."

Malcolm laughed at his friend. "Okay, you keep telling yourself that. It'll make you feel better when you see them together."

"I appreciate the concern, bruh, but you might want to take a look around."

Malcolm stopped the hamburger headed toward his mouth. "What's that supposed to mean?"

Quentin smiled slyly. "That means, I see someone by the tent that may make you 'wanna hang back'."

Malcolm looked closer and saw Abril standing with Imani, Raegan, Trent and G.

"Whatever, man. I'm good."

"If you say so."

***

"Mmph. She's gained a lot of weight."

"Shut-up, Mani. You can be so critical." Raegan rolled her eyes away from Imani.

"Well, she has."

Morgana walked up just then and hugged her old friends. "Everyone looks great."

Imani glanced around again. "Not everyone."

"Why are you so bitter?" Abril looked over at Imani.

"Because I spent the last ten months starving myself and what do I see when I get here? I'll tell you what, a herd of cows."

"Um, girlfriend, that's on you. Nobody told you to starve yourself."

Imani stood at the table listening to Abril while piling her plate high with food.

"Really, Mani? You need to eat the whole tray?"

"I said I been starving for the last ten months. I'm hungry, shoot."

"Okay, but don't say anything when you can't fit into your dress tonight."

Imani placed a small portion of the food back into the tray. "Fine, but we're hitting the Waffle House in the morning."

Quentin walked up just as Stacia and Richard were leaving. Stacia turned around after she'd gone a few steps.

"Um guys, I forgot to grab a napkin. Can one of you hand me one, please."

Quentin handed her the napkin he was holding, but made sure he touched her when he did it. Then he made sure to prolong contact. Richard noticed the touch and took a step toward her.

"You got it, baby?"

His voice snapped Stacia out of whatever wormhole she had fallen into.

"Uh, yeah, thanks."

She and Richard walked silently to their table and sat down.

"Ex-?"

Stacia looked up guiltily. "What makes you say that?"

Richard swallowed his food and wiped his mouth before he continued speaking.

"Well, for one thing, he hasn't taken his eyes off of you since he arrived and for the other, nobody takes three minutes to hand over a napkin."

"That was not three minutes."

"Oh, yes, my dear, it certainly was. So, is he your ex-?"

Stacia glanced over in Quentin's direction. "We were friendly, once."

Richard followed her gaze. "I need more friends like that."

"He's not your type."

Richard grinned. "Easy, kitten. I got a man. Besides, that one only has eyes for you."

"So you say." Stacia didn't want to admit it, but Richard's words stirred up hope she thought was long gone.

"Me and the rest of the people under that tent say. Is that what I'm doing here, making him jealous?"

She shook her head slightly. "You are here to escort me to my twentieth college reunion and no other reason."

"So you always bring your gay, second cousin-clients to events like this and let everyone think you're dating said gay cousin?"

"You could have told them any time you wanted."

Richard smiled wider this time. "And miss that little show you put on back there? Oh no, honey. Even if I hadn't broken a sales record yesterday, that little display you and your friend just exhibited was worth the trip. Don't worry, sweets. Your secret is safe with me. If for nothing else than I'm expecting more drama from you two tonight at the gala."

***

Abril left the restroom and turned left to go back to the tent where her friends were sitting. She absolutely did not plan to run into Bryan. Not right then, but she did. She literally ran into him.

"Abril?"

Dang. "Oh, hi Bryan. How are you?"

He looked shell-shocked. "I'm really good. How about you?"

"I'm great."

He nodded, still not over the collision. "You look good."

"Thanks...well, I guess I better..."

"Hey, how's Jade?"

"She's good, really good. She'll be starting her senior year in college in a couple of months."

A genuine smile appeared on his face. "Wow, junior year, already."

Abril returned the smile. "Well, she did get a head start."

"That's right. Driven, just like you."

"I guess so."

"Tell her I said..."

"I will and I really need to get going, but you take care."

"Thanks. You, too."

Abril hurried away from the man as fast as she could without running.

***

Quentin looked up just in time to see Abril walking away from Bryan. He looked over at Malcolm and pointed, "Hey, isn't that the guy Abril ended up with after she broke up with you?"

Malcolm turned around to see the two figures going in separate directions, but he didn't turn away. "I couldn't tell."

"Uh, bother, you should be able to read dude's license from here, the way you're staring him down."

"Doesn't matter. She made her choice."

"Choice? Man that was twenty years ago. Besides, they're not together any more."

Malcolm folded his arms and settled back. "Like I said, she made her choice. She replaced me."

Quentin looked over at his friend. Some things would never change. "She repaid you. Get your facts straight. You dished it out like a champ, now you can't handle it?"

Imani met Abril a few steps away from the tent with a cold bottle of water.

"Was that Bryan?"

Abril glanced over her shoulder. "Yeah, he's aged well."

Imani handed over the bottle and laughed. "He didn't have a choice. He was gorgeous twenty years ago. Man... his lips, and don't get me started on those eyes... oooh girl!"

Abril looked as if she would throw up. "Ugh, don't remind me."

"Well, did he at least ask about Jade?"

"Yeah, he did. And that's something, I guess. I wish it could have ended better, for her sake."

"Does she ever ask about him?"

"Not since middle school. She took it really hard when he left."

Imani reached an arm around Abril's shoulder. "Well, that's to be expected. He was her world for the first eight or nine years of her life."

"I know, I just... I tried to overcompensate when he left and I shouldn't have done that."

"Abril, you did a phenomenal job with her by yourself. Look at how well she's doing now. You're fine and she's fine and I'm sweaty. Let's go get out of this heat and rest up for tonight. You know we've got to squeeze a lot of partying in, in a short amount of time."

***

"Hey, mom."

"Hey, baby. How are you doing?"

"I'm good. Just tired of studying."

Abril switched her cell phone to the speaker option and continued painting her fingernails. "I bet. Are your exams over yet?"

"Yes, finally! I finished the last one yesterday afternoon."

"Good! And I'm not even going to ask how you did because I know you aced everything."

"Yeah, they weren't too bad. So what are you up to?"

"Well, we had a picnic earlier and tonight is the gala. By the way, all of your aunties and uncles said hello."

Jade grinned from ear to ear. "Aww. Tell them I said hey and I love them."

"I will do that. So what are you up to now that school is out?"

"Well, I'm going out with some friends."

Abril knew her daughter well. She was rarely without a boyfriend. "Some friends or a friend?"

"It's a group of my friends that want to introduce me to one of their friends."

"Well, what's he like? And what happened to the last guy, what was his name?"

"Who, Derek? That's been over."

Abril laughed, remembering all too well the angst teenagers go through while dating. "All right, well have fun, but remember what you're there for."

"I will, mom. By the way, did you see…"

Abril nodded. "I saw Bryan and he asked about you. He told me to tell you hello."

Jade was quiet for a moment. "Oh. How is he?"

"Looked to be fine. Baby, I need to finish getting ready, but have fun tonight and be careful."

"Okay, mom. Love you."

"I love you more." Abril blew a kiss into the phone and hung up. She shouldn't have rushed Jade off the phone so quickly. She knew the girl was only searching for more information on Bryan, and by extension, herself. Abril sighed. "I'll have a good long talk with her the next time she comes home."

***

"Wow, it's beautiful in here tonight." Morgana looked around what used to be the cafeteria of the centuries old college. It had been completely transformed by lights, streamers, and balloons hanging from the ceiling. Signs and posters, popular twenty years ago, hung on the walls.

She still hadn't seen Keith yet. Earlier, she overheard a couple of the guys say that he was coming tonight. She couldn't wait. She had bought every flattering thing she had seen in the store last weekend. Diana, bless her heart, could barely keep up. One thing was for sure, though; Diana would have a line of new suitors following her around after

28

church service tomorrow. A new hair-do and a few key pieces, along with a makeup tutorial showed Diana to be the beauty Morgana knew lay underneath the dowdy clothing.

Morgana spotted Abril near the refreshments and went to join her.

Abril looked up as Morgana approached. "Did you see Ethan Graves?"

Morgana turned to look at her ex-boyfriend of twenty years. "Yeah, I saw him and his wife when I came in."

Abril shook her head. "If someone had asked me, I would have put money down and said that you and Ethan would have been married right after we graduated."

Morgana smiled wistfully. "Yeah, that was a long time ago. People grow up and minds change. What can I say? Have you seen the rest of the group?"

Abril shook her head. "Not yet, I just got here. I was about to start walking around."

Morgana placed some appetizers on her plate as Abril tried to speak over the music.

"Good, I'll join you."

Abril looked up and smiled. "Maybe in a few minutes."

"Why?"

"Well, don't look now, but Mrs. Ethan Graves is making a bee-line right for you."

Morgana shook her head. "Gotta love a jealous woman. Go tell Ethan he's welcome."

Abril thought she misheard her friend. "What?"

"Go tell Ethan he's welcome, and hurry up, this won't take long."

Abril walked away moments before Mrs. Graves came to stand behind Morgana. The woman said nothing for a while, just stared at what used to be her competition. After some time, she finally tapped Morgana on the shoulder.

"Excuse me. Are you Morgana?"

She turned around and smiled her brightest smile. "Hi, yes. Were we in some classes together? Forgive my memory, it's terrible."

"Uh, no. I'm married to your ex-, Ethan."

Morgana's eyes grew wide with confusion. "Who?"

Mrs. Graves, who had been savoring the thought of this confrontation ever since they booked tickets for this reunion, was taken aback. "Ethan Graves, your ex-boyfriend."

Morgana looked sad for the other woman. "I'm sorry, I don't remember. So much gets crammed into twenty years, you kind of lose track of the details, you know?"

"Um, yeah, I guess so."

"Well, I hope you and...what did you say his name was?"

"Ethan."

"Right, sorry. I hope you and Ethan enjoy the rest of the reunion. By the way, you should try the shrimp balls. They're really good."

"Thanks." Mrs. Graves walked away from the refreshment table unsure of what had just happened. Morgana met up with Abril in the middle of the room.

Abril laughed as she saw Morgana approach with a sly grin. "How'd it go?"

Morgana shrugged her slim shoulders. "I took care of the situation."

"Good, and Ethan said thank you."

"Thanks."

Abril reached out and grabbed her arm. "Come on, I found the fellas."

Morgana laughed thinking about the old nickname for the guys. "The cinder-fellas."

"Yep. They're over here."

"Is Malcolm with them?"

Abril stopped and turned to face Morgana. "Of course he is."

"Have you talked to him?"

"No." Abril said the word curtly, almost defiantly.

"Abril, don't you think you should at least try?"

"Look, I know what you're thinking, but I'll be headed back to Denver in the morning and life will go back to normal. "

Morgana took her friend's hand. "Okay, but you're still in love with him. You need to deal with that."

"No, whatever I felt for him died a long time ago. It took a while, but I got over him. I'll deal with other things as they come up."

"All right, I hope you know what you're doing."

"I do. Everything is fine. Now, let's go sit down and see our friends."

Abril had indeed found the group. She led Morgana straight to the table where they sat down. Quentin sat with Malcolm, Trent, and Garrison "G" Reaves. Imani and Raegan had joined them earlier. The only persons missing were Keith and Stacia.

Morgana walked toward the table with a smile on her face. She had seen Stacia. Keith was the one she was hoping would show soon. She wasn't disappointed when moments later, Keith appeared.

Quentin was the first to greet him. "What up Reverend!"

"Hey, man." Keith distributed hugs and handshakes around the table. When he got to Morgana, the hug lasted a second longer than the other hugs. A quick kiss on the cheek and a quiet "Hey, baby" whispered in her ear justified last weekend's shopping trip in her mind.

"Why is it, that the worst ones always become preachers?" Malcolm looked up at Keith with a smirk and a smile.

Keith smiled back. "Maybe it's because we know we needed the most help."

Malcolm nodded. "Yeah, some of us needed a lot of help. "

Keith nodded back. "And some of us haven't realized it yet."

Malcolm rolled his eyes. "Hey, I got all the help I need. I'm living the life. You with me G?"

Garrison shook his head. "Nope, speak for yourself. I turned my player card in years ago. I grew up."

Keith turned to look across the table. "G, brother, where's the wife?"

Garrison ran his hand over his head. "Uh, yeah. That didn't pan out."

Imani wasn't surprised. She told him that little gold digging girl was no good from the beginning, but he acted like he couldn't hear her. She finally stopped saying anything all. Two months later she heard he had married the girl through the grapevine. That was almost four years ago and they really hadn't spoken since then.

Trent just laughed. "Didn't pan out? Alrighty, then." He raised his champagne flute in the air. "To ex-wives!"

All the men except Malcolm raised their glass and joined Trent in the toast.

Malcolm scoffed at his friends. "And y'all are getting on me? All grown up, huh?"

Trent took a swig of bubbly before setting his glass down. "Face it Mal, man. Part of growing up is getting married."

Malcolm looked around the table. "And I guess part of growing up is alimony and child support too, right? You can have that. Is anybody at this table married anymore?" Malcolm looked around the table again. "That's what I thought, all grown up? I grew the hell up, and I got the bills to prove it."

Garrison raised his glass again. "I hear that. We all got those, man."

Keith grabbed Abril's hand and pulled her onto the dance floor. Morgana saw the move but wasn't upset. He was the only one who hadn't seen Abril yet. Besides that, he was Jade's godfather. They had a lot to catch up on.

The rest of the friends laughed and talked for a while until Garrison noticed that the group wasn't complete. He looked around the room.

"Something's missing, or should I say someone."

Raegan leaned back in her seat and looked at Garrison who had just sat down. "Would you be talking about Stacia?"

"Yeah, where is she?"

Imani looked across the room. "Oh she's here." She nodded in the general direction. "Sucking all the air out of the room with that fine ass man of hers."

All the ladies expressed their assent with a murmured chorus of 'Mmmhmm's'.

Quentin clamped down on his jaw and Garrison rolled his eyes. "Well, that's not right, is it? I mean, we haven't seen her in what, ten, twenty years." He gave Quentin a glance before standing up. "I'll be back."

Imani sat up, at attention. "Aww, snap! It's about to get interesting."

Trent looked over at Quentin when Garrison left. "You all right with this?"

Quentin squared his shoulders. "All right with what? It's been twenty years and if you haven't noticed, Stacia is grown."

Trent nodded. "Oh, I noticed." He said it before thinking and received a quick jab in the ribs by Raegan.

Malcolm looked across the room to where she was sitting. "Every brother up in here has noticed." When Quentin looked as if he would start swinging at any moment, Malcolm shrugged. "I'm just saying."

Keith and Abril finished dancing and tried to catch their breath. "Hey, you want to get some air before we go back?"

Abril fanned herself vigorously and moved her head up and down in time with the new song just beginning to play. "Yeah, let's go."

They stepped outside into the college courtyard and walked around. They stopped in front of Keith's old dorm.

Abril looked up into the night sky and then at the imposing building. Her voice was quiet. "You ever stop to wonder what would have happened if only we'd made different choices?"

Keith looked up with her. "I used to, but then it dawned on me that I couldn't change the past. That's when I started concentrating on the future."

Abril sighed. "I know, it's just..."

"Hey, everything turned out all right. We're fine. Jade is fine. Life is good. Let's just leave the past in the past."

She nodded. "You're right, as usual. Let's go inside. I'm thirsty."

Garrison returned to the table a few minutes later with Richard and Stacia in tow.

"Everyone, I know you remember Stacia, and this is Richard.

"Hey, guys." Stacia said it bashfully while she made eye contact with mostly everyone at the table. Quentin only nodded but everyone else gave her a warm smile and a friendly greeting.

Raegan pulled out an empty chair next to her. "Have a seat, you two. There are some empty chairs over here."

Stacia smiled again. "Thanks. Hey, where are Keith and Abril?"

Malcolm inclined his head forward. "Right behind you."

Stacia spun around to see Keith and Abril walk up. She reached her arms out for a hug. "Hey, your ears must have been burning. I was just asking about you two."

Keith gave her a hard squeeze. "And here we are."

Abril hugged her next. "Hey, honey. How's the company doing? Last time I saw you, you were in Essence magazine."

Raegan smiled. "I know, all dolled up and looking like the consummate business woman. How is it?"

Stacia beamed proudly. "It's crazy, but I love it. Wouldn't change a thing."

"Let's dance." Richard spoke in Stacia's ear roughly, but loud enough for everyone at the table to hear him."

Stacia looked up bewildered. "All…right."

He grabbed her arm with more force than he needed to, and pulled her onto the dance floor.

Everyone at the table was left with their mouths open. Quentin turned in his chair to look at his friends, hoping he had just imagined the scene. Everyone was still in shock. Everyone except Imani, that is.

"Oh, hell no!"

That was all the justification Quentin needed. He stood up and took one step. He didn't get far because Keith laid a heavy hand on his shoulder. Quentin turned back to look at his friend.

"What are you doing? Did you just see that?"

Keith nodded. "I did, but I need you to calm down first."

Quentin was nowhere near calm. "But he just…"

"We saw him." Trent had gotten up a half-second after Quentin. "But Keith is right. If you ruin this night for Stacia, it would be worse than doing nothing at all."

All the guys were standing now. Malcolm put his hand on Quentin's shoulder. "Take a minute, and a couple of deep breaths, then walk over and calmly ask to cut in. There's no harm in talking."

Garrison nodded. "Right. And if after that, the brother still needs his ass kicked, you can count on us."

Malcolm palmed Quentin's shoulder once more. "All of us."

Keith downed the rest of his drink. "Amen."

Stacia was beyond upset. Dancing in a sea of people, she whispered angrily to Richard. "What do you think you're doing?"

He looked down at her smugly and grinned. "I'm getting you your man. What does it look like I'm doing?"

"It looks like you're about to catch a beat-down."

"But I didn't, because cooler heads prevailed, like I knew they would."

Stacia looked across the room at the five men standing in a semi-circle. "That has yet to be determined."

"Okay, I was a little worried, but listen. Your guy should be over here in about two minutes. I'll be gone before then, but when he asks if you need a ride home, you take him up on it."

Stacia was still confused. "But…"

Richard wouldn't let her continue. "And when he asks you for your phone number, give it to him."

"But…"

He kissed her forehead. "No buts. Now go get your man." He walked off and left her standing in the middle of the floor. She stood alone and staring after him. Stacia turned slowly, still trying to figure out what Richard was up to when she made her way to the edge of the dance floor. Two steps away stood Quentin with his hand extended toward her.

He led her gently back to the dance floor. They danced for several moments to the slow song without speaking. He took a deep breath to steady himself. He didn't want to appear angry when he spoke. He was, of course, but not with her.

"Please tell me you're not involved in an abusive relationship because I really don't think I could handle that right now."

Stacia looked up at the handsome face in awe. She had waited twenty years for this moment. Now that it was here, she couldn't speak.

"Stacia." His voiced snapped her out of the paralysis.

"I'm not involved in an abusive relationship. I'm not involved in a relationship at all. He's…a friend."

Quentin stopped dancing to look down at her. "Are all your friends crazy?"

She laughed like she hadn't in years. She missed him. "Only a few of them. And what about you?"

"What about me, what?"

38

She looked up, unsure if he was free to be with her right now. "Last I heard, you were married."

He looked off for a moment, but then back at her. "Yeah, well. Turns out she wasn't the one for me. All I have is friends, right now."

Stacia smiled. "Like me."

He looked around the ballroom. "Speaking of friends, where is Bizarro now?"

"Oh, he had to leave. I guess I'll need a ride back to the hotel."

Quentin leaned down and spoke into her ear. "I got you."

"Thanks."

They finished the dance then slowly tore away from each other and headed back to their friends.

"Hey you two, you're just in time." Malcolm raised his glass and the rest of the table joined in.

"Here's to the Super-Friends. We were supposed to change the world, but..."

Trent touched his glass to Raegan's. "Hey, we're healthy, and we've got jobs to take care of our bills."

Keith lifted his glass higher. "And that's a lot to be thankful for right there."

"Amen." Morgana clinked her glass with everyone's.

"To the Super-Friends."

"To the Super-Friends."

Chapter 3

"Well, that was a bust." Morgana started her car and listened to the engine run. "I got more attention from Ethan's wife than Keith."

She locked the car doors then took a look around to make sure no one was around ready to car-jack her. She bowed her head and said a quick prayer. "God, I'm turning all this over to you. If you want Keith and I together, then please make it so that we will end up together. If we're not supposed to be together, make that happen, too. Amen."

She pulled out of the garage and headed home. "At least I got to see the girls."

***

Quentin parked the rental car and looked over at Stacia. "You ready?"

Stacia undid her seatbelt. "You really don't have to walk me up to my room."

He didn't answer her until he walked around to the other side and opened her car door. He took her hand to help her out. "Yes, I do."

They crossed the lobby of the W Hotel and entered the elevator.

"By the way, you look really nice tonight."

Stacia actually blushed. She was still getting used to being this close to him again. "Thank you. You look rather dapper, yourself."

When the doors slid apart he reached for her hand. "We're going to stay in touch this time, right?"

"Yes. Absolutely."

She tightened her grip on his hand and nodded as she led him down a corridor for several yards. They stopped in front of her room. They were there only a few seconds when her room door swung open and Richard glared at Stacia.

"Oh, you decided to come back."

He completely ignored Quentin, glared at Stacia once more and walked away. The door didn't close completely so they could hear Richard getting ice and pouring himself a drink. Quentin stared at the door in unbelief for several moments. He started to open the door to find out what Richard's problem was, but stopped when he felt a delicate hand on his chest.

"Don't." She could barely get the word out because she was laughing so hard.

"You know you're not going back in there, right?"

She pulled him away from the door. "I told you, he's just a friend. It's not what it looks like."

Quentin was unconvinced. "Just a friend, huh? What are you doing bringing a friend to the reunion anyway? All your friends were already here. I mean, if you had just..."

"Shut up and kiss me."

He stopped mid-sentence. "What did you just say?"

She moved closer and raised her face up toward his. "I said kiss me."

He didn't need to be told a third time. His right hand caressed her cheek and his thumb moved gently over her bottom lip. He hadn't touched her like this in over two decades, so he relished every moment. He took his time remembering the curve of her jaw line, the smoothness of her skin, the sparkle in her eyes, and how her nose turned up at the end. He loved how she glowed under the soft light. He felt the pulse at the base of her neck with his other hand and noticed how it sped up. He took one step closer so that she was pressed between him and the wall. When he had her where he wanted her, he slowly lowered his lips until they touched hers. He lingered there a moment, not moving but enjoying the contact.

He deliberately began to nibble and tease her mouth until she was squirming with anticipation. Just when she thought she couldn't take anymore, he opened his mouth wide and engulfed her. His tongue found hers seconds later and it was all she could do to stand up straight. He had his way with her mouth then slid his tongue down her neck. He worked his way back up and slipped his tongue into her ear. She almost passed out but strong arms held her securely.

"I missed you." He whispered the sentiment into her damp ear. Her heart was swimming. Her mind was screaming. Her hormones were scrambled. She was totally and completely off balance. She hadn't seen him in twenty years, but if he had asked her, she would have followed him anywhere and done anything. Her hotel room was right here or she would go to his, anything to make her body stop aching.

I haven't seen him in twenty years. What am I doing? She shook her head to try and clear it. It would have worked if she hadn't looked up to see his mouth moving toward hers again. She didn't know if she could take another round but she was willing to try. She closed her eyes, parted her lips and waited for his tongue to meet hers.

"Stacia, can I see you for a moment?" Richard's voice felt like a bucket of ice water thrown on her soul. Quentin took a deep breath and tried to get himself under control.

"Something is not right with that dude."

Stacia shook her head and leaned forward until it touched his chest. She didn't know whether to run into the room and kill Richard or thank him. She was out of control and Richard's voice, however unwelcome, snapped her back to reality. She took one more gulp of air and grabbed his lapels before kissing him quickly once more. "Will I see you in the morning?"

"Absolutely, but my plane leaves at noon so I won't be able to make it to anything they have planned for tomorrow."

"My plane leaves about thirty minutes after yours, so how about breakfast?"

He nodded. "Breakfast sounds good, but it's just you and me, right? Bizarro isn't coming?"

She laughed lightly. "No. His flight leaves at six, tomorrow morning. He won't be a problem."

"Good. I'll call you in the morning." One more kiss and he was gone.

Stacia stepped into the hotel room and closed the door behind her.

"You have a death wish don't you?"

Richard barely glanced at her as he flipped through a magazine. "I was helping you out. You were about to blow it."

"How was I about to blow it?"

Richard sighed and closed the magazine to deal with the slow learner before him. "You never listened well. Grandma Jacy was right when she said 'why buy the cow when you can get the milk for free'."

Stacia took a step into the room and studied her cousin. Maybe Quentin was right when he said something wasn't right with Richard. Maybe her dear cousin really was going crazy.

"First of all, I am not a heifer. Secondly, plenty of couples stay together after having sex first. Some of them even get married. Not that I'm saying I want to get married, but it happens."

Richard stood up and walked to the mini-bar. "First, I've known you since birth so I can attest to the fact that you are indeed a heifer. Secondly, I wouldn't say plenty. I would say some. Some men get married to the same woman after having sex with her and a lot of those are not in love, just tired of looking for the perfect arm piece. Thirdly, look around honey, you are forty-two years old and you're married to your business, which if you haven't noticed, doesn't do a great job of keeping you warm at night."

The reality of Richard's words washed over her. She sat down on the small loveseat against the wall and sunk into it. He was right. After her divorce, she threw herself into her business. As much as she loved her work, it couldn't help with lonely nights or solo appearances at family events.

"It would never work, even if I wanted it to. Chicago and Paradise Hills, Nevada aren't exactly conducive to a long term relationship."

Richard returned to his chair after satisfying his late night urges with a snack.

"One step at a time, please. You two obviously have unfinished business that you need to take care of, so first things first. You want him thinking about you when his plane lands in Chicago, tomorrow. Now, thanks to me, that will happen."

Stacia grinned. He was probably right. "But that doesn't mean it will turn into something bigger."

Richard shrugged. "You never know what can happen in twelve months."

***

Trent opened his hotel room and peeked down the hall. It was quiet and empty. He raced down the hall in his pajama bottoms and knocked on a door. He waited a few moments and when no one answered, he knocked again. Raegan opened the door, yawning and half asleep.

"What?"

"Come on baby, let me in." He kissed her quickly as he pushed his way into the room.

"You really didn't have to wake me up."

He backed up and wrapped his arms around her. "I'm sorry baby, but I was with G. and you know that brother likes to hang."

She nodded and yawned again. "I know. It's just that I have an early flight tomorrow."

"I told you that you should've booked our flights at the same time. Come back to bed. I missed holding you."

He led her to bed and climbed in beside her.

Her breathing became even and he thought she had drifted off back to sleep. He was wrong.

"You know I caught that comment about Stacia earlier this evening, don't you."

He groped through the covers for her hand and brought to his mouth. After he showered it with kisses, he pulled her closer. "That was just commentary. Besides, you don't have to worry about us. I've only got eyes for you, and she's only got eyes for Q."

Raegan smiled in the dark. "I know. I hope they get their stuff together. Twenty years is a long time."

"It is, but they're not the only ones."

***

The cafeteria turned ballroom was almost empty. Keith and Abril sat at a table as she caught him up on her and Jade's lives.

He smiled like the proud godfather he was. "I'm so proud of her."

Abril smiled back. "Me, too. I wish she could come home for the summer, but I'm glad she knows what she wants and she's going after it."

Keith became quiet for a moment. "Have you told her about..."

46

"Malcolm." Abril was surprised to see him standing right next to her when she looked up.

He smiled. She hadn't changed much. She still had the most adorable expression when she was shocked or surprised.

"Sorry, didn't mean to surprise you. I just wanted to know if you two wanted to go out."

Abril looked over at Keith. "Um, I don't think so. I have an early flight in the morning. I need to get going."

Malcolm took off his dinner jacket and pulled out a chair. He was going to try his hardest to convince Abril to spend some time with him. She loved him once, but he had walked through most of his life with his eyes closed. He knew he should have treated her better back then, but he was just a boy. He was a stupid boy more focused on pleasing himself than anything or anybody else.

"I can take you to your hotel, if you'd like."

She shook her head. "I'm staying with my aunt."

He smiled. He had always liked her aunt. "I remember. I can take you."

She shook her head again. "Thanks, but Keith said he would take me. It was good seeing you, though. Tell your Granny I said hello, and take care of yourself."

"Yeah. You, too."

Malcolm walked away. She obviously didn't want him near her. The way she just dismissed him told him that. Abril used to be so sweet. She used to always make time for him. Then, all of a sudden, she just changed. He wished he knew why, but he wasn't about to sit around and wait to be rejected until the answer revealed itself.

***

"The next stop is concourse A. A as in alpha." The recording that is the voice of the Atlanta Hartsfield International Airport transit system informed all the passengers of their next destination. Stacia looked up at Quentin.

"I guess that's me."

He nodded, trying not to show the sadness he felt. He lifted her chin for one final kiss. "I'll call you when I get in."

"I thought you were getting in before me."

He shook his head. "No, remember I told you that I have a layover and mini business meeting this afternoon."

"Oh, yeah." Her eyes sparkled when she thought back to when he told her that very thing. He was nibbling on her neck right after he picked her up this morning. "I must've been distracted."

The doors to the indoor train slid open, but she was able to slip in one more embrace before she walked onto the platform. Quentin watched her until the train pulled out of sight. He barely noticed the thin gray haired man that got on the train right before Stacia got off. The older man took a seat near where they'd been standing and watched the exchange between Quentin and Stacia.

"Saying goodbye to your sweetheart, huh?"

Quentin turned to see the old man sitting behind him. "Yeah, I guess so."

The man nodded with understanding. "I don't know how you do it with traveling and all, but if you got a good one don't let her go. I was married for forty-four years."

"Was?"

The man smiled generously. "Yes, my sweet Ethel lost her battle to pancreatic cancer late last year."

Quentin's complete focus shifted to the man. "Oh, I'm sorry."

The man stood as he heard his stop called.

"Don't be. She lived a good full life. We raised four great kids and had time to spend together after retirement. That's what it's all about, you know. Fallin' in love again when all the distractions are gone." The doors of the train slid open and the man grabbed the long handle of his suitcase. "Take care, son."

Quentin shook the old man's hand as he left the train. "Thank you, sir. You, too."

He pondered the man's words for the next few moments until the recorded voice broke into his thoughts.

"The next stop is concourse C. C as in Charlie."

***

Malcolm looked around the entire kitchen for the spatula. He had already scrambled the eggs and poured them into the hot pan, but he couldn't find anything to flip them. He hadn't cooked in his own kitchen in years. He opened one cabinet drawer and then another. In the last cabinet he saw something he didn't expect. He reached all the way into the back of the cabinet and pulled out the long forgotten bottle of wine.

He set it on the counter then walked away. He came right back and stared at it for longer than he should have. He hadn't had a drink in almost five years. It was like finding a long lost friend... except this friend betrayed him, almost to his death. He reached for the bottle but stopped when he heard the doorbell. He opened the door and saw someone he didn't expect to see.

"Keith? Man, what are you doing here this early? Aren't you supposed to be in church or somewhere else besides here?"

Keith held out the dinner jacket that Malcolm left at the gala the night before. "I'm on my way to church now, but I wanted to drop this off first."

Malcolm took the jacket from his friend. "Thanks. Come on in. You got time for breakfast?"

Keith stepped into the house. "Sure, but it smells like you burned it already."

"Oh, shoot!" Malcolm ran back to the kitchen as fast as he could in sweat socks on polished wood floors. "Whew, just caught it. Almost forgot about the eggs." He turned around to look at Keith who was looking at the bottle of wine on the counter.

Keith took his own jacket off and sat down at the breakfast bar of the large granite island in the center of the kitchen. "Looks like I'm just in time."

Malcolm's brows drew together of their own accord. "Just in time for what?"

"To save you from burning your eggs, of course."

At least he didn't try to lecture him. Keith may have turned into a preacher, but he was still cool in Malcolm's book. Malcolm used a wooden fork to tend to the eggs, then opened the bottle of wine and poured it down the sink. "So, is Abril gone?"

Keith poured some orange juice into his glass out of the carafe Malcolm set out earlier.

"Yeah, her plane took off about an hour ago."

"That's good. It was good seeing everyone. Everybody looked great."

Keith had to agree and his thoughts were on one body in particular. He should have gotten Morgana's number last night. He should have gotten it when he saw her a few weeks ago but he didn't. He knew she was involved in church now, but he wasn't sure he was ready to jump into another relationship, especially with someone he called a "friend".

***

Imani pulled into her driveway and turned off the radio. She decided to stay over last night and come back this morning since the drive between Atlanta and Birmingham was only two hours. She gathered her things and headed into the house. Once inside, she looked around. It seemed so empty. She really should get some more friends. *Some local ones would be nice,* she mused. Seeing your friends every five years couldn't be healthy, no matter how much the friends were committed to the relationships.

She plopped her bags down and headed for the kitchen. *What am I thinking? I've got friends.* There was the girl at work, Anne. They spoke almost every day. And then there was the guy down at the coffee shop. He always had a smile for her in the mornings. And what about the girl down at the bank? They always spoke to each other. *What is her name...Chanice. No, it was closer to Charise... or Chantice, that was it.*

51

Imani sighed as she reached into the fridge for a cup of yogurt. It wouldn't be so hard making friends if her mouth weren't so big. And it's not that she had a big mouth specifically, but she definitely had opinions. And opinions were meant to be shared, at least that's what she thought for most of her adult life. Once she left home and had the liberty to express herself freely, she didn't stop. She didn't stop when anyone's feelings got in the way or even when her own job was at stake. Which was why she was on her fourth firm in three years. She always told the truth. And she would continue to do so.

***

Quentin looked over to his left and noticed that the frequent fliers were starting to form a line in order to board the flight. They probably had another five or ten minutes before the gate was opened, but he stood up as well. He took his place in the line against the wall closest to the jet ramp. People he recognized from the reunion had been walking by all morning. His former classmates, along with their spouses and children filled the airport.

He recognized one guy as someone he noticed at the class of '86 reunion tent. The man recognized him, too, and made his way over.

"Hey, you were at the reunion this year, right?"

Quentin shook the man's hand. "Yeah, twentieth. I'm Quentin."

"Gary, and it's my twenty-fifth. Nice to meet you. We sure know how to throw a party don't we?"

Quentin smiled. "Yep, always have. You come by yourself?"

Gary set his carry-on bag down at his feet "Yeah.

I'm not the marrying kind. At least, that's what my ex-wife told me."

"Same here." Quentin had heard those exact words before. He smiled when he thought back to the woman who divorced him. But her face was quickly replaced by Stacia's and his smile grew wider. "I think I may be ready to try again, though."

Gary shook his head violently. "Don't do it. You're going to be sorry three months later."

Quentin laughed. "So what? You're just going to ride off into the sunset, solo?"

Gary raised his thick shoulders. "Hey, somebody's got to do it. Might as well be me."

"So, in thirty years...?"

Gary stepped back to do a little two-step with himself. "There will be single ladies at the old folks home and I'll just be getting started. We can put some Usher on. He'll be an oldie by then."

Quentin shook his head and slapped the man on the back. They had just called his section to board the plane. "Good luck with that."

Gary grabbed his bag off the floor. "Hey, I'm not the one who needs luck. If you're thinking about getting married again, especially at this age, you are the one who needs all the luck."

Quentin nodded. "I'll take my chances. See you in five years."

Chapter 4

"Where are you going?" Jade's roommate, Callie, called out as the door was closing.

Jade popped her head back in and grinned. She'd been doing a lot of grinning lately. Her new boyfriend was absolutely perfect. The chemistry was phenomenal. It had only been a couple of days, but he had already told her he loved her, several times.

"I'm spending the night with Davis. I'll see you in the morning."

Callie shook her head as the door closed shut. She loved Jade like a sister, but the girl had serious issues. She was never without a man. And she always seemed to fall for the ones who were no good for her. The Davis that Jade was so in love with, was a completely different guy than the one who showed up at frat parties and disappeared with two girls at a time.

"I hope she figures it out soon."

***

"Mr. Calder?"

"Yes, what can I do for you, Ms. Thomas?"

"Well, you could look up."

Malcolm was so busy going over the paperwork

on his desk that he hadn't looked up in hours. When he finally did, he noticed that it was dark outside and the clock on the wall read eight. He also noticed Lana Thomas in lingerie and a trench coat.

"What are you doing, Lana?"

The low, sultry voice almost purred with satisfaction. "I thought now would be a good time to get some work done."

Malcolm looked her up and down. "In your drawers?"

"I just thought, well, since we were so good together last time, we could do it again."

Malcolm set his pen down and studied the young woman. She was certainly attractive but for some reason, he hadn't been himself lately. If he were honest, he would say that it started after seeing Abril. Something about her always got to him. Even though they broke up over twenty years ago, there was something in him still trying to get back to her. Three weeks after the reunion and it was only Abril's face that filled his dreams now.

He tried to tell himself that it was psychological. Malcolm wanted to think that the only reason he wanted her so badly was because she had brushed him off, but he knew better. He had laughed at Quentin but the truth was, he admired what his friend had done. Quentin corrected the mistake he had made over twenty years ago and now he was back together with the woman he loved.

Malcolm sighed. The lovely young woman in front of him offered an easy out. He could fulfill his sexual needs and psychological needs all in one shot. All he had to do was paste a mental picture of Abril over Lana's body and he could leave, a happy man. The problem was, he just wasn't up for it tonight.

"Lana, look, what you offered last month was nice, but it won't be happening regularly. Since you're new to the company, I should probably lay down some ground rules. And really, there's just one, but it's a big one. That rule is Thou Shalt Not Try To Get Thy Hooks Into The Boss, understand?"

"Yes." She nodded numbly.

"Good. If you want to sleep around with half this company, that's your business. And you should know that, like me, most of the men will take you up on it, but I hired you based on the experience and qualifications listed on your resume. If you can't handle the job or perform at the level I'm expecting without spreading yourself across a desk every night, tell me now."

"No, no, I can handle it. I just thought..."

"What, that you had to sleep your way to the top in this company?"

"Well, yes. I'd heard that you were...'

"Lana?"

"Yes?"

"You should quit while you're ahead. Now, I expect you here tomorrow morning at eight o'clock, ready to work, and in appropriate business attire."

"Yes, sir. Thank you, sir."

***

"I miss you." Quentin couldn't be happier. Once he determined that Richard, the nut she brought to the reunion would be no problem, he decided to move forward. The love of his life was back in his world and he was going to do everything in his power to keep her there.

Stacia laughed. "You just saw me three weeks ago."

He leaned back and adjusted himself in the bed. He loved to hear her laugh. In fact, he had fallen in love with everything about her, all over again. "I know, but I really miss you. When am I going to see you again?"

"Well, I've got two projects I need to finish up by next week, but I may be able to clear some time at the beginning of next month."

His smile became even broader. "Good, I'll start making plans."

"What kind of plans?" She wanted to know.

"I don't know, I was thinking of a long weekend on a nice island somewhere.

Stacia's mind went to the last time she experienced tropical winds and gorgeous sunsets, and she swooned slightly under the sway of an imaginary breeze. "Well, we're too late to plan for Independence weekend, but I can get away at the end of the month."

"The end of the month sounds good. Now, the next question is St. Thomas or St. Maarten?"

Stacia's philosophy was 'you have not because you ask not'. She didn't see any reason to change things up here. "How about both? Let's do a cruise."

"A cruise." He said the words slowly. "I like the way you think. I'll have my travel agent start looking tomorrow."

Stacia thought about Abril and would have loved to send some business her way, but she wasn't ready to let anyone know what was going on just yet. She at least wanted to make sure they still got along the way they used to. "Sounds good. So, what's the rest of your week look like?"

Malcolm visualized his day planner and realized he was in for a busy week. "Taking it easy for a few days, then I have to fly to Dallas on Wednesday to meet with a new client.

"Dallas? Isn't that where Trent lives?"

"Yeah, he's actually the one that set me up with this new client."

Stacia nodded. It made sense. They always looked out for one another. "Okay, and make sure you holler at Raegan while you're there, too."

Quentin was about to move on with the conversation when he caught what she said.

"I thought Rae was in Phoenix."

"She was, but she moved last year when she got her promotion."

"All right. Text me her number and I'll make sure to call her while I'm there."

***

Trent raised his glass in a congratulatory toast with Quentin's. He'd reminded Raegan this morning to leave work on time so she wouldn't be late. He'd been with her long enough to know she wouldn't remember, whether he reminded her or not. He'd been here, alone with Quentin, for almost an hour.

"Thanks again for introducing me to Kevin and his company. I think we're going to work well together."

Trent raised his hand in a fake salute. "Hey, man, no problem. Just don't forget, I work on commission."

58

Quentin laughed. "Always the business man. All right, you got it." He finished his second round of drinks and looked around the restaurant. "I wonder where Raegan is? I told her we'd be here at six-thirty."

"Oh, the traffic from that part of town is crazy this time of day." He tried to say it casually, but no one ever accused Trent of having a poker face.

Quentin glanced at his friend suspiciously. "Really? So, you two see each other often?"

Guilt was written all over his face. He didn't want to lie to his friend, especially since he felt like, for the first time in his life, he was involved in a real relationship. He was proud and wanted everybody to know it. On the other hand, he wanted to respect Raegan's wishes, too.

"No... I mean, well... You know. Here and there."

Quentin nodded. "I see."

Trent was relieved. "You do?"

"Yeah, how long you two been hooking up?"

Man, Rae is gonna kill me. He shook his head. "It's not like that. We might actually be going somewhere."

Quentin was surprised but he had to admit, they had the right idea. "So why not let everyone know when we were at the reunion?"

"I don't know. Just wanted to keep it between us a little longer, I guess."

Raegan finally sauntered up to the table. "Hi, you two. Sorry I'm late. Traffic was horrible. So, how've you both been?"

"He knows." Trent delivered the words without a hint of an apology.

Raegan shrugged. "I guess it had to come out sooner or later."

Quentin pulled out a chair for her. "Hey, trust me, I'm not mad at you. In fact, I'm happy for you both. So happy in fact, that I might be following in your footsteps."

Raegan smiled knowingly. "How is Stacia? I haven't had a chance to talk to her since the reunion."

"She's good. We're supposed to be getting together soon."

Trent gave him a pat on the back.

"Good. I never thought I'd say this, but relationships are a good thing. I highly recommend them."

Raegan slid closer to Trent. "Me, too."

Quentin waited for the waiter to bring Raegan's drink and take everyone's order before he continued. "Yeah. I think I got married too young last time. I wasn't sure who I was or where I was going but now..."

"You're ready to try it again?"

He bobbed his head in Raegan's direction to answer her question. "Yeah, I think so."

"We're with you, bruh. No need to explain it to us."

"I know man, I'd be preaching to the choir. But at least you two are on the same page. I still need to convince Stacia."

Raegan reached across the table to encourage him. "Somehow, I don't think you're going to have much of a fight on your hands."

"Really?" Quentin was ready to grab onto the

slightest sliver of hope, no matter how thin.

"Really. Now, if it were Imani or Abril, I'd say don't waste your breath. I'm not even sure where Morgana is, but after our conversation the other week, I think Stacia is ready."

Quentin wasn't ready to exclude the others. "But that's the thing, I think Abril and Morgana, and especially Imani, could use a good relationship right now."

Trent recognized the look on his friend's face. He had seen it before. "You look just like you did twenty years ago, before you orchestrated our first panty raid. What are you thinking?"

"Come on, look at us. We're all successful, with good heads on our shoulders. And we're all alone."

"Hey, speak for yourself."

"Well, you two are off the market now, and hopefully Stacia and I will be soon, but that leaves the rest of our friends out there, blowing in the wind."

Raegan listened with active interest. She had always enjoyed a little matchmaking back in the day. And who better to help than her friends. "And you think we should be the ones to try to get them together?"

Quentin looked at Raegan like she wasn't thinking straight. "Think about it. Do you really want to be around Imani at the next reunion when we have somebody and she doesn't?"

Raegan shuddered at the thought, then she laughed out loud. "No, I guess not. And it might actually work."

Quentin was confident. "Of course it will work."

61

Trent wasn't as convinced, but he meant what he said earlier about relationships. Everyone deserved a good one. "Well, we've got three single men and three single women."

Raegan nodded in agreement. "That's an even number."

"Right, and like us, they aren't getting any younger."

Raegan smiled brightly when a thought popped in her head. "You know, homecoming is right around the corner."

Quentin nodded again. "Yep. October will be here before you know it."

Trent raised his glass. "Let's do it. Let's do a super-sized hook up, super friends style."

***

Jade bent over the toilet for the third time that evening. She heaved one final time and the entire contents of her dinner dropped into the already murky water below.

Callie stood in the door. "Jade, are you sure you're okay? Maybe you should go to the infirmary."

She shook her head in an almost imperceptible move. "No, it's probably just a bug I picked up. I'm sure it will be fine by tomorrow. I'll just sleep it off."

"Okay. If you're sure?"

Jade offered a weak smile. "I am. You go ahead on your date."

Callie backed away, looking worried. "All right, but call me if you need anything."

"I will. I promise."

When Callie finally closed the door behind her, Jade pulled out the small plastic stick with a pink plus sign. She was clearly pregnant. After the first positive test, she ran back out to the drugstore and purchased two more. One test may have been questionable, but three couldn't lie. She had to face the fact that she had gotten herself pregnant. *Well, I had a little help.*

But, that was where the help ended. Her loving and devoted boyfriend disappeared soon after hearing that he was going to be a father. They'd been together all of six weeks. She told him as soon as she'd found out, but he didn't take it well. He changed his cell phone number and avoided Jade like the plague. She hadn't seen him in a couple of weeks, and she hadn't told anyone else yet.

She carried a positive pregnancy test around with her everywhere she went now, like an omen. It was silly, but it did help her deal with the reality of the situation. She'd been staring at the thing for a month and a half. In that time, she did a lot of self-examination. She also came to a few conclusions.

First, she was going to keep her baby. Jade couldn't deny that the option of abortion sounded good to her. But her mother had kept her when she was in the same situation, and she wanted to provide that same opportunity for her unborn child. It would be hard, but she knew if she just worked a little harder, she would be able to raise the child by herself.

Second, she would wait to tell her mother about the baby until after it was born. As much as her mother preached about the dangers of going down the same road, she had done it anyway. She knew her mother would be disappointed. But she reasoned that telling her mother would go much more smoothly with a cute, gurgling baby in her arms. She had already lined up a part-time job to start saving money. Everything would be fine if she wasn't so tired all the time.

***

"A cruise, huh?"

Stacia looked at Richard and smiled. "Yes. Quentin and I are going to get reacquainted."

Richard was dubious. "That's fine. Just remember what I said. He booked two cabins right?"

"Yes, father."

"You're joking, but I'm right. You always want to leave them wanting more. That means no sex for you."

Now it was Stacia's turn to look doubtful. Five days under a tropical sky, in some of the world's most exotic locales and no touching one of the sexiest men on the planet?

"I don't know…"

Richard simply shook his head. "Oh, ye of little faith. Haven't I been right so far?"

Stacia thought back over the last couple of months. "Now that you mention it, yes."

He swatted her across the head with a rolled up newspaper. "That's because, I know what I'm talking about. If he's really interested, he'll do what he needs to do to get you. In the mean time, now would be a great time to clarify what you really want."

Finely plucked eyebrows came together in confusion. "What do you mean?"

Richard sighed again. One day his pupil would understand. "Well, if you're making him wait, at least be clear on what you're making him wait for. Do you even know what you want?"

She leaned back in her chair and thought about it. They could just keep things going the way they were. She was enjoying herself and she knew he was, too. She had a feeling, though, that Quentin wanted more. She wanted more. But was withholding sex the way to get it?

Richard was right, however. She needed to get clear on what she wanted. But what if he didn't want more. What if he had no marriage plans in his future? Where would that leave her? She knew where. Exactly where she was before, and she'd had enough of that place. She would try Richard's way and see where it led. At this point, she had nothing to lose.

**

Malcolm splashed cologne on his face and headed back to the bedroom. Seeing Abril at the reunion had shaken him, but he bounced back. It was okay if she didn't want to spend time with him. He was an attractive man, making excellent money and living in a city full of women. He knew of several women who would kill for the opportunity to spend a night with him. He could probably find a few in his phone book if he tried.

But if the reunion showed him nothing else, it showed him that he needed to move on. Abril had moved on a long time ago. He was a little slow in catching on, but he knew how to get back in the race. All he had to do was find a woman he liked. He might actually learn to love her, later.

His date tonight was the first step. He figured it

shouldn't take more than a couple of months to find someone he was compatible with. He wasn't even asking for a lot. He was looking for someone who was attractive, with a good head on her shoulders and some common sense. How hard could that be?

The woman he was seeing tonight worked in his firm's legal department. She was pretty enough with a good sense of humor. He had picked her because she had been eyeing him for the last several months. It always helped when they were more interested in you. He probably wouldn't have given her a second glance on the street, not that anything was wrong with her. She just wasn't the type he was normally drawn to.

He adjusted his tie as he stared at himself in the mirror. He was game for anything once. He would try it. What did he have to lose?

Well, it's worth a shot, but... she looks nothing like Abril...

***

Dinner was divine. Freshly caught lobster tails with prime rib and butter-roasted asparagus, along with the lightest chocolate mousse cheesecake she'd ever consumed. Stacia sat cuddled next to Quentin in a booth near the back of the ship's auditorium. The huge boat rocked gently back and forth on the night waves as the entertainer for the evening crooned ballads from a long forgotten era. She was in heaven.

When Quentin reached down and stole a kiss, Stacia had to hold on to her heart. If she didn't, she would have handed that over, too. He whispered something in her that she couldn't hear, but it didn't matter. She felt it all the way to her toes. The singer finished two more songs then sent them off with an old classic, *The Way We Were.*

They sauntered hand in hand, through the lobby and up to the deck where their cabins were located. He didn't say a word until he reached her cabin door, and then only after he had thoroughly kissed her good night.

"Goodnight, lovely."

"Goodnight, handsome."

He moved forward, until there was no room between them. "You know, you could invite me in for a night cap."

She shook her head, mostly to clear it. "No, I can't. Remember what we talked about. This is a get reacquainted trip only, and that's all it is."

His lips extruded in a fake pout. "You don't trust me?"

She ran her thumb across his lips and let it linger. "You aren't the one I'm worried about."

"Oh." He was so caught up in the sensation of feeling her hand on his mouth that he completely missed the meaning behind her words. The realization hit him a moment later.

"Ohh." He took her hand and kissed it before placing it on his chest. "So, I was wondering?"

"Yes?" She sounded breathless and she knew it.

"Where do you see yourself in five years?"

She tried to hide her disappointment. She wasn't exactly sure what she expected him to say, but that definitely wasn't it. She took a deep breath and tried to focus.

"Well, my business should be completely established by then, so, I guess I'll be focusing on my personal life."

"Your personal life, and what does that look like five years from now?"

He had removed her hand from his chest and was drawing tiny circles into her right palm with his thumb. She was trying to concentrate on an answer, but she felt herself falling into the abyss all over again.

"Stacia?"

"Hmm?"

"What does your personal life look like five years from now?"

"Um, I suppose I'll be a wife and a mother."

He nodded his approval. "A wife? A wife is good. And to be one of those... you're going to need a husband."

She smiled, only now remembering how he used to tease her with his words. She missed that about him. "I suppose I will."

"And this husband of yours. What's he like?"

She smiled broader, now realizing where the conversation was headed. "Oh, he's great. Strong, level headed, and very attentive to me and the kids."

He returned the smile. "He really does sound like a great guy."

"Yeah, he's okay."

"Just okay?" He brought his lips within millimeters of hers. The sexy rumble of his voice made her quiver inside. He raised both hands over her head and held them there before he kissed her again.

***

Trent watched Raegan as she fixed dinner. She

had pretty much moved into his home and he didn't mind one bit. If anyone had told him that he'd be in a serious relationship when he was over forty, he would have laughed them out of the place. But, looking at Raegan now, Trent couldn't imagine life any other way. It almost scared him, the depths of his feelings for her.

He settled in his mind, right then, that he would make her his wife. He had heard her say, some time ago that she never wanted to get married again, but he was on a mission to change her mind. And he would do it.

***

Malcolm cleared the dishes on his grandmother's table and placed them in the sink. He had grown up in this house, as had his father. The little house was worn, but still full of Granny's love. When his parents were killed in a car accident caused by a drunk driver, Granny didn't hesitate to take him in and raise him.

His parents had started a small college fund already, but it wasn't much. She used the money from their life insurance policy to pay for the rest of his education. That didn't leave a lot of money left for her to raise him with but she managed. She always did. His granny was the only family he had left in the world. He didn't appreciate her when he was younger, but the older he got the more he recognized her for the gift she was.

He had asked her several times to move in with him, but she always shooed him away. She preferred her own house, and she wasn't shy about letting him know it. She was still spry and alert, but she moved a lot slower than she used to. That's why he called her and checked on her as often as he did.

"So, you never told me how the reunion was, honey. Did you see many of your old friends?"

Malcolm continued cleaning the table but answered her hurriedly. "Uh, yeah. Everybody was there."

"Oh, that's nice. How is that sweet girl you used to date during your first few years? What was her name, Gabby?"

"Abby. And she's fine. She was there."

Granny smiled in remembrance. "Now that was a great girl for you. I knew it from the moment I laid eyes on her. You should've brought her by."

Malcolm never looked up, just kept moving. He wasn't comfortable talking about Abril. Her rejection still hurt. "She was busy."

"I see. Boy, why are you so agitated?"

He hesitated for only a moment. "I'm not agitated."

Granny's glassy green eyes narrowed to focus in on her only living relative. "You most certainly are agitated. Now sit down."

Malcolm finished putting everything away and then came to sit in front of her. He was never sure how she was able to read him like a book, but she did it every time.

"Honey, look, you're older and wiser now. Nobody's going to blame you if you feel the need to reevaluate some things. If you're looking around at things in your life that need adjusting, then just do it."

"Just do it. That's easier said than done."

"No, baby. Staying the same is the easy part. It's pushing out of the rut you carved for yourself that's hard. Trust me. I know."

***

Keith picked up the phone and put it down again for what had to be the hundredth time. What if Morgana wasn't interested? What if he tried and she shot him down. He had known her for over twenty years. He actually considered her one of his closest friends, even though they didn't talk often.

She just had the kind of personality that you wanted to be around. She was fairly easy-going and fun to be around most of the time. She could have her moments, but she was definitely the kind of woman you should hang onto.

He saw Ethan eyeing her at the reunion, and if he wasn't mistaken, there was regret in the other man's eyes. Keith could hardly blame him. Even after twenty years, Morgana was still turning heads. The only question in his mind was if she wanted to be with him. They weren't getting any younger, so getting together now would essentially mean forever.

When she showed up at his church a while back, he almost jumped up out of the pulpit to greet her. He wasn't sure why the greeting after the service didn't come across as intensely as he felt it. Maybe he was scared. He eyed the phone once more. Maybe he should just leave it alone. She looked happy.

***

Garrison shifted in his seat slightly. He knew his son was winding down his part of the conversation. He hated that he couldn't see him as often as he wanted, but he also recognized that it was his fault. He had completely destroyed his marriage to the point where his ex-wife wouldn't deal with him.

It wasn't his fault entirely, but he knew he shouldered the blame for most of it. The decisions he made, acting single while married, didn't build a strong foundation. He figured it out when she packed up and moved two states away, taking their only child with her. He was able to talk to the boy every day, but it wasn't the same. Add that to the fact that Imani was probably right about the marriage being doomed from the start, and he wasn't surprised that he was alone.

Garrison sighed and hung up the phone, not sure what to do next. If his family were still here, he'd just be finishing with bath time and preparing to check for monsters under the bed. There was nothing to do now but check the locks on the doors and veg out in front of the T.V. He kicked himself at least once a day over the mistakes he made. Of course he knew better now, but it was too late to change things. Reconciling was out of the question because she was engaged to someone else. He promised himself though, that if he ever got another chance, he wouldn't mess it up.

***

Stacia woke up smiling. It was the last day of the cruise, and so far, it had been the best trip ever. She lifted her left hand so that the sun hit the sparkling rock on it. She wanted to make sure that last night wasn't a dream. Quentin had slipped the ring on her finger after getting down on one knee in the middle of the dining room. Stacia was surprised but, as he

72

reminded her later, he had known her for twenty years. He wasn't going to take another twenty trying to get reacquainted. She agreed to marry him amidst the cheers and applause of her sailing companions.

She was sitting at breakfast now, waiting for him to finish at the buffet. When he made his way back with a full plate, she waited for him to get settled.

She raised her hand to block the rising sun and its light from doing damage her eyes. "Okay, so what's so important that we needed to meet this early?"

"Still not a morning person, huh?" He stuffed some waffles in his mouth and waited for her answer.

"Not so much."

"Then, I apologize for getting you out of bed at this time of morning, but we have important business to discuss."

She knew they had a lot to discuss about their upcoming nuptials, but she thought all those details could wait, at least until they reached land. "Business, like what?"

"Like our friends."

"What about our friends?"

"Well, did you know that Rae and Trent are together?"

"I had my suspicions" she nodded.

"Oh." That one caught him off guard. "Well, the three of us were talking when I was in Dallas about the rest of the group."

"And...?"

"And we think the others would benefit from

hooking up, too."

She smiled. "We, huh?" Quentin hadn't changed a bit in twenty years. He was always a schemer, plotting and planning ways to shake things up.

"Okay, mostly me, but I'm right. Those six are just three hook-ups waiting to happen."

Stacia pondered his words. "And how do you plan to make that happen?"

"Easy." He flashed his brilliant smile. "Homecoming is about three months from now. We announce our engagement and then let nature take its course, with a little push from us."

"So, we announce our engagement at homecoming and then tell our friends that the four of us have been scheming for the last few months to hook them up with each other? Oh, that sounds great. Then we can sit back and watch them fight it out, gladiator style."

"You don't think it's going to work?"

Stacia shook her head emphatically. "I'll give you one out of three. Keith and Morgana I can see happening pretty easily, but Garrison and Imani? Come on, and don't even get me started on Abril and Malcolm. Do you know what opening that can of worms will do?"

"Come on. It's been twenty years. Jade will be out of college in a minute. Don't you think it's time Malcolm found out he has a daughter?"

She sighed heavily. "If it were up to me, he would have known a long time ago, but I'm not the one he put through hell and then dismissed after being caught with another girl in his bed."

Quentin grimaced. "She did take that pretty

74

hard."

"As she should have. She was completely in love with him and for him to treat her the way he did... I just don't think we should push Abril too hard, that's all."

He understood. Malcolm really could be an ass sometimes. "All right. We have a few months. How about you start warming her up to the idea. You know, just drop his name in conversation every now and then and see what happens."

"Okay, I'll try it." Stacia still had misgivings, even after agreeing to do it.

***

Malcolm paid the check and waited for his date to return to the table. He was ready to go home, alone. He thought sure this girl would be better than the chick from the legal department. All she wanted was sex.

Apparently his name had been making the rounds at the office as a must try ride. He was completely fed up by that point, so he gave her what she wanted. He put on a condom, turned out the lights and pretended she was Abril. He let her have twenty years of pent up frustration in one night, and he still wasn't satisfied. He knew he wouldn't be until he got what he wanted.

When he walked her to the door after he was done, all she kept saying was 'oh, my god, oh, my god'. He should have figured it would have made the office gossip worse, and it did. He now received daily visits from women who didn't work in his department. A couple of them didn't even work in his building.

He thought this girl would be different though, because she really looked the part. She was his type from head to toe, but it wasn't right. She wasn't a good fit. She wasn't what he wanted. *Her smart mouth didn't help matters any.* Plus, she was a little on the young side. *Pity,* he thought, as she walked toward the table. She really was quite attractive.

"Sorry, that took longer than I thought."

He smiled graciously. "No problem at all. I've already taken care of the bill."

False eyelashes lowered, seductively. "So, did you want to come to my place for drinks, or should we go to yours?"

He wasn't moved. "Actually, I don't drink anymore. Besides, it is getting late and I have to be in the office early tomorrow."

"Look, if this about that comment I made earlier about older men…"

Malcolm smiled benignly. "No. It's just that I think we're at two separate stages in our lives right now. Two different mindsets"

She finished the last of the wine in her glass, as she looked him over. "I see. Well, I know where my mind is. Where is yours?"

He thought about it a moment. *Somewhere, in Colorado with a woman who won't give me the time of day, anymore.* But, he never said it out loud, only rose to escort her to her car.

Chapter 5

"Congratulations on your engagement, honey!"

Stacia smiled brightly. "Thanks, Rae. It's going to be fun telling everybody next month."

"I know. I can't wait to see their faces."

Stacia laughed lightly. "I can't wait to see their reactions when we unveil this cock-eyed scheme of ours."

Raegan laughed with her friend. "One thing is for sure, the evening will be pure entertainment. You didn't tell Malcolm, did you?"

"Are you kidding? It would be over before it started. As far as he knows, he's hosting a homecoming party, and that's all."

"Okay, just checking."

"I'm still worried about it, to tell you the truth."

Raegan agreed. "I know. I am, too. But it's been twenty years. Let's throw the cards up in the air and let them fall where they may."

***

One month later, cool October air settled over the peach city and ushered in those coming home. The group attended a football game that afternoon, then separated to rest up for the party later that evening. Raegan, Trent, Quentin and Stacia arrived at Malcolm's house early to set up. He helped for a little bit, but eventually left them to go shower and change.

Quentin made sure he heard the water running in Malcolm's bathroom before he began to speak.

"Okay, everybody know what they're doing?"

Stacia was still worried. "Are you sure this is a good idea?"

He walked over to where she was hanging streamers and wrapped an arm around her shoulders. "Come on, baby. Don't you want our friends to be as happy as we are?"

"Of course I do. I just don't want any of this to blow up in our faces."

He gave her a solid squeeze and picked up the streamers near her feet. "It'll be fine. We just need to remember not to let everyone else know that Trent and Raegan are already together."

"And that we need to keep Abril away from Malcolm."

"Right. I take it she didn't warm up to the idea of him during your conversations the last few months?"

The smirk on Stacia's face said it all. "More like ran cold. She changed the subject every time. And why are Rae and Trent acting like they're not together?"

"We don't want everyone else to feel like they're being ambushed. So Trent and Rae are going to act as facilitators tonight. You know, just help to move things along."

Ten minutes later, the doorbell rang and the rest

of the friends started to arrive. Abril was the last to get there and Stacia went to open the door for her. Abril was slightly shocked when she stepped into the expensive home. She had no idea Malcolm was living this well. She removed her coat slowly and took her time taking things in. The house was beautiful, but even if she'd known he was living like this, she wouldn't have told him about Jade. There are some things money can't buy.

"Wow, nice place."

Stacia looked around. "Yeah, Malcolm did okay for himself, but then we all did."

Abril nodded. "Yeah, I guess we did, some better than others. You really didn't have to pay for my ticket here, you know."

Stacia reached out to hug her long time friend. "Yes, I did. I wanted my girl here, and I know you have extenuating circumstances."

Abril hugged her back with a chuckle. "Is that what they call it now?"

Malcolm descended the stairs just as they released each other. "I thought I heard voices out here. I'll take your coat, Abril."

"Thanks. Is there a powder room around here?"

Stacia turned slightly and pointed down a hallway. "I think there's one right down there."

Malcolm cleared his throat quickly. "Uh, actually, there's one right behind you, Abs."

He was rushing and really hadn't meant to say her old nickname. It just slipped out. But, judging by the look on her face, it must have brought back the same old memories for her that it did for him.

Almost all of the friends called her 'Abs' at one

point or another, but it was different with Malcolm. When he used to call her that, he was usually touching her abs in some intimate way. She pushed the old memories out of her mind as best she could and looked at him with her best blank stare.

"Thanks, again."

When she had gotten settled and joined the others, they talked for a few moments and put some food on their plates. Quentin let them get seated before he wandered to the front of the room.

"Hey guys, thanks for coming. I wanted to make a quick announcement."

Garrison looked up from his seat at Quentin. "Aw man, sit down. This is a party."

"I know it is, but I wanted to let you all know that I made a pretty serious decision recently. I decided to take the plunge... again. I'm getting married."

Everyone in the room froze. No one spoke or moved until Stacia went to stand beside Quentin. "He probably should have said, we're getting married."

The room exploded with cheers and applause. Everyone jumped up to congratulate the happy couple. Keith was the first to speak.

"It's about time! We thought you two were never going to get it together."

Everyone laughed, including Stacia. "It took us a while but we managed to get there."

Quentin smiled down at his fiancée. "Yeah, we did."

"What made you jump after all these years?" Imani wanted to know.

Quentin cleared his throat. "Honestly, it was the reunion. When I was leaving, I ran into a guy who was there for his twenty-fifth year. He was single and happy. Even talked about picking up women in the old folks home, which is fine if that's what he wants. But I didn't want to be that guy."

Raegan bobbed her head up and down, solemnly. "Yeah, I hear you. We blinked and twenty years went by."

Quentin raised his glass in her direction. "Exactly, and I didn't want to make the mistake of letting another twenty go by without this beautiful woman in my arms. So, here's to a better second half than the first. And, I wish you all the same happiness."

When no one said anything, Raegan walked behind Trent and nudged him. He opened his mouth and said the words like he was reading from a script. "I would love to find the same happiness."

Everyone turned to look at Trent while Raegan tried to stop her eyes from rolling at the bad delivery. It was quiet and she thought she was going to have to speak out again, but Keith saved her.

"I would, too, honestly. I had to visit a church member in the hospital last week. She was completely alone. I mean she had no one visiting her."

Morgana felt sorry for the woman. "That's so sad. I don't want to end up like that."

Imani agreed. "Me, either."

Stacia touched Quentin's arm when it seemed that everyone's mood was dropping. He put forth a simple directive. "So, do something about it."

Garrison looked perplexed. "What do you mean do something about it?"

Quentin looked at everyone in the room eye to eye. "Well, look around you. I see an even number of unmatched singles who've known each other for over twenty years. You don't want to be alone for the rest of your life, but do you really want to hit the dating scene again, and at over forty years old this time? I'm just saying..."

Garrison glanced over at Imani. "I'm just saying too, all of us aren't compatible."

Stacia spoke up. "Maybe not, but I think your options are better in this room than what you're going to find out there."

Quentin tried to bring her in for a homerun. "Think about it guys, we have seen the best and worst of each other over the last twenty years. But the choice is yours. If you want to go out there and get to know somebody new, and hope it works out, good luck with that."

He left them to ponder his words as he walked over to the bar. Trent joined him a moment later.

"You're, uh, laying it on kinda thick, aren't you?"

Quentin smiled confidently. "Watch and learn my friend. Watch and learn."

"All right, I'm in." Keith had stood up and looked back at Quentin. He hoped no one saw his eyes veer toward Morgana.

"Me, too." Morgana smiled and thought she saw Keith relax a little, but she couldn't be sure.

"I'm in." Trent was calmer, sensing an end to the charade.

"As am I." Raegan beamed.

"What the hell." Imani shrugged."

Garrison acquiesced. "Right, what the hell."

Several moments passed and every one turned to look at Malcolm. "What? I'm not the only one who hasn't said anything."

Abril took a deep breath and jumped. "Count me in." She didn't want to do it because she didn't want to take the chance that she would end up with Malcolm. But what they were saying made sense.

Malcolm looked around the room, trying to avoid Abril's gaze. "So, let me get this straight. Just because we've known each other for twenty years, we're all supposed to get married and live happily ever after in la-la land. Doesn't that sound a little too cut and dry to anybody else besides me?"

Quentin knew Malcolm would be the one to stir up dissension in the group, but he also knew that Malcolm wanted Abril back. He just hoped the bait was alluring enough to reel him in. But with Malcolm, a little extra effort was always required. Like now, reverse psychology was needed to push him over the edge.

"Nobody's twisting your arm, man."

Raegan started doing the math in her head. "But, that would throw the count off. We'd have one of us without someone."

"I could go either way, tell you the truth." Imani chimed in. "So, if Malcolm doesn't do it, I'll step out to make the numbers even."

Malcolm thought about the next reunion, and seeing Abril with one of his best friends was not an option. "Fine, I'm in."

The women gathered on one side of the room while the men gathered on the other. Stacia shook her head. Some things would never change. They continued talking for several minutes until Abril thought about the logistics of the situation.

"So, how are we going to do this?"

Quentin walked back to the middle of the room. "Well, if you already know who you want to be with, you can just start picking teams."

Morgana's face wrinkled up. "Picking teams? Like we're about to play ball?"

Keith locked eyes with her. "Well, we are, kind of."

Garrison sat back in his chair. "Well, you know what they say. Ladies first."

Imani stood up, incensed. "Unh-unh, no. That's your job. You need to just stand up and say what you want."

Garrison looked at Quentin. "See, that's what I'm talking about right there. Lack of compatibility."

"Oh, I got your compatibility!"

Of course the ladies took Imani's side and insisted that the men say what they want. The men, led by Malcolm, stood with G. The group had worked themselves up to a fevered pitch until Stacia put two fingers in her mouth and made a shrill, sharp whistling noise.

"People! Please! If you don't want to do it that way, we can just draw numbers. It's not rocket science."

Raegan eyed Trent. "Okay, numbers sound fair."

Trent nodded. "Yeah, numbers will work."

Quentin followed Stacia to Malcolm's home

office where they made the numbers to be drawn. She looked over her shoulder to make sure they were alone. "I hope you know what you're doing."

Quentin wasn't quite as sure as he sounded. "It's going to work out fine." But he was hopeful.

"I sure hope you're right. They were almost at each other's throats back there."

"I know, but I really think it's just the guys bravado being stirred up. They're nervous, so what we're getting right now is fight or flight. Once they calm down, it will be fine."

"Okay."

They walked back into the living area and set the ceramic bowls that normally held paperclips down on the coffee table. Trent and Raegan were the first to line up and the others followed suit. Once all the numbers were pulled, the men and women separated back to their respective corners.

Raegan turned quickly when Trent cleared his throat. He pretended to drop something and knelt down. She tried to stifle a laugh when he settled into a catcher's position, as if he were on a baseball field. He pointed two fingers straight to the ground and raised his thick eyebrows while looking directly at Raegan. She saw him and went into action, looking over her girlfriend's shoulders until she found what she was looking for. Raegan grabbed the number two out of Imani's hand before she realized what was happening.

"What the...? Hey!"

"Imani, please." Raegan whispered. "I don't want to travel to God knows where, when Trent is already in Dallas with me."

Raegan received a roll of the eyes with her number. "Fine. Take it."

Keith caught Morgana's eye next. He held up four fingers straight in the air and began to flip them back and forth quickly. Trent tried to get up without being seen, but he was too late. Malcolm saw what Keith and Trent were doing.

"Oh, y'all flashing signals now? What the hell is that?"

Keith cleared his throat. "Uh, I was just praising the Lord."

G. looked over at his friend with a deadpan expression. "With your thumb down, man? I don't even go to church and I know that requires all five fingers."

But it was too late. Morgana was already switching numbers with Abril.

"May I?"

Abril just laughed and shook her head. "Go ahead."

"Thank you, Abby!"

Malcolm looked at Garrison "You need to flash somebody, too?"

G. looked between Abril and Imani. "No, I'm good. I got number three."

Abril blew out a huge sigh of relief. "Me, too."

Malcolm was so upset he could hardly breathe. The only thing he could do was glare at Abril. "Fine, it's me and Imani, then."

"Oh, joy." Imani grabbed her drink and sat down. *God, please, if you get me out of this, I promise I'll never do anything wrong again, ever.*

***

A few hours later, the ladies met at Houston's Restaurant. All but two of them were in shock. Morgana's was a happy shock, but she was still shocked. Judging by Keith's reaction to her at the reunion, she barely even put on makeup tonight. She was more than surprised when he began flashing her signals at Malcolm's house. They exchanged phone numbers before they left. All the new couples did, but she definitely planned to question him later about his sudden interest in her. She looked around the table at the rest of friends. Most of them seemed to be in shock, like her.

"Did we really just agree to do that?"

Imani did a half snort. "Unfortunately, but I didn't sign a contract, so it's not binding. Malcolm can start acting crazy if he wants to. I'll roll out with a quickness."

Abril looked worried. "But are we sure this is a good idea?"

Raegan shrugged her shoulders. "I don't know, but I do know Quentin was right. We say we don't want to be alone, but do we really want to jump back out there? I know I don't."

"Exactly." No one saw the clandestine fist bump that occurred under the table between Raegan and Stacia. "At least we know these guys. We know what we're working with." She looked around the table at each of her friends. She was almost sure that everyone was on board for the long haul. "Abby, what's that face for?"

"Just thinking I guess. I went to England last year and while I was there, I ran across an article about couples sleeping together before marriage."

When she didn't go any further, Raegan prompted her. "And?"

Abril took a bite of her meal and continued. "It just mentioned that couples who wait until after marriage to have sex, have a better relationship because it forces them to communicate on a deeper level. They take that into the marriage."

Morgana nodded in agreement. "Yeah, I had already planned to do that, but strictly for religious reasons."

"You're celibate?" Abril was surprised.

"Yep." Morgana nodded again.

"For how long?" Imani wanted to know.

"Years." Morgana confirmed.

"Get outta here." Raegan was skeptical.

"No, really."

"Me too, guys." Stacia spoke up

"Since when?" Imani suspected Morgana to say something like that after her religious conversion, but Stacia?

"Right before I started this relationship, and honestly I needed some convincing by my cousin, but he was right. Why do you think Quentin scheduled the wedding so soon?"

Imani's surprise turned into a smirk. "So you tricked Q into marrying you?"

Stacia shook her head. "No. I just stood by my principles and he made up his own mind."

Raegan's eyebrows shot up. "Wow. That's pretty serious."

Stacia shared her opinion. "I know, but after listening to my cousin, I did some thinking. I had tried the other way before, and look what it got it me. And don't get me wrong, I love my divorce lawyer but that's not the way I had planned for things to end between Edward and I. We were in bed before we had our first real conversation, and we paid for it."

Abril nodded in agreement. "I was thinking the same thing. Sex takes over the relationship and after a while it becomes the only way you communicate. I know what didn't work for me. I want to try something new now."

"Well you know what they say," Morgana raised her glass. "To get something you've never had, you have to do something you've never done."

Abril raised her glass. "I'm in."

Morgana touched her glass to Abril's. "Me, too."

Stacia joined in the toast. "Likewise."

Raegan hesitated. "Um, I'll try."

Imani raised her glass, but she didn't touch theirs. She took a swig instead. "We'll see, but I'm not making any promises. Actually, you know what, it's Malcolm. I can definitely make that promise with Malcolm."

Chapter 6

Morgana laughed at Keith's joke. They'd been on the phone for the last three hours getting reacquainted.

"Very funny, but you never answered my question."

Keith had a feeling he knew which question, but decided to ask anyway. "And what question is that?"

"How is it that you barely looked at me when we ran into each other several months ago, showed absolutely no interest at homecoming, didn't contact me for several months after homecoming, and then flashed me a signal at Malcolm's?"

"Look. I... I just didn't know if you were feeling me. We hadn't really spent any time together in over twenty years, and I'm heavily involved in church now. I just didn't know if you were interested. I was always interested, even back in school."

"You were?"

"Yeah, but you were with that Ethan guy, for almost our whole four years. There was no point in even trying back then."

She had to acknowledge the truth of that

statement. "I guess you're right."

"Whatever happened between you two anyway? I thought for sure that you two were headed for the altar."

Morgana thought back. "We just didn't see eye to eye on some things."

"Okay. Well, how about we get together for dinner next week?"

"That sounds nice."

"Good. There's a place downtown on Piedmont that I really like. I'll send directions to your phone. We can meet up after work and have a nice dinner on Monday."

"Sounds good."

***

Imani came into her house and dropped her bag and briefcase on the floor. Today had been a crazy day and it would have been nice to have someone to talk to. She had been handling things by herself for so long, that she was ready to share her life with someone. She had kind of hoped it would be Garrison that she got matched up with, but since he didn't feel the same, whatever. She glanced over at the phone sitting on the counter. *Malcolm has lost his mind if he thinks I'm calling him first.*

***

Malcolm glanced at the phone on his desk. Abril could have said she had a different number, or at least not look so relieved that she didn't have the same number as him. The computer screen blinked with a message and he shut it off. He could have gone home earlier but what was the point? No one was there waiting on him. He fast-forwarded his mind ahead five years to the next reunion. *If Abril thinks she's going to show up with Garrison at the next reunion, she's dead wrong. Garrison wants Imani anyway, he was just too scared to say so.*

The thought occurred to him that he and Garrison were in the same boat the other day. They probably could have saved everyone a lot of trouble if they'd just done like Imani suggested and stood up and stated what and who they wanted. It didn't happen the other day, but Malcolm determined within himself that he would make it happen, and soon. He would do what he needed to do to get his life straight and bring Abril back into it.

***

Abril hung up the phone with her last customer for the day. Garrison had called her earlier, but she was too busy to take the call. She had so much going on, but one thing she was thankful for is that her number didn't match up with Malcolm's number. She wasn't sure what she would have done if that had happened. How could she tell him that he had a college-age daughter that he never met and never knew existed? How would he even handle it? She almost told him once or twice when Jade was much younger, but she always stopped herself. She convinced herself that Malcolm wasn't ready to know. *He's probably enjoying life as a bachelor. He probably has no time for a child anyway.*

***

"Wow, your baby bump is growing."

Jade laughed and rubbed her stomach. "I know. The doctor at the clinic said she's healthy and growing well, but she's a little small."

Callie shook her head in amazement. "I don't know how. You've been eating everything in sight."

Jade faked a pout while her roommate laughed. "Hey!"

"You know it's the truth! That baby has a right to be twelve pounds when she comes out."

Jade smiled and rubbed her rounded belly again. "She's going to be a delicate flower."

Callie slipped on a coat and walked to the door. "I'm sure you're right. Call me if you need anything. Lord knows you can't call your no good, baby daddy."

"No, I can't."

"I still can't believe he just disappeared. Who transfers schools to avoid being pinned with paternity?"

Jade shrugged. "Boys with rich parents and good lawyers."

"I guess. But I'm serious. I can be back over here in twenty minutes. Call me if you need anything."

Jade put her hand over her heart. "I will. I promise."

***

Malcolm descended the stairs of his large, immaculate home. He hadn't worn his old work clothes in what seemed like forever. He walked down the same hallway that he had stopped Abril from walking down a few weeks ago. After a couple of steps, he opened the door to a room that contained no light. To anyone who didn't know any better, it would appear as if the room was painted completely black. A closer look would reveal that it wasn't black paint on the walls, but charred drywall.

He set his tools down on the floor when he heard the doorbell. A few moments later, Garrison and Keith stood with him in the burnt room. No one spoke for a minute.

Malcolm turned to look at his friends. "I didn't think you two were coming."

Garrison didn't hesitate. "It's his fault," he said as he pointed to Keith. He looked around the room again. "Man, I didn't remember it being this bad."

Keith looked around as well. "Me, either. How long has it been?"

"About five years," Malcolm admitted.

Garrison took off his Jacket and threw it into a corner. "And the insurance company covered every other part of this wing of the house, except this room?"

Malcolm picked up his tools from floor and walked further into the room. "No, they would have, but I kind of felt like I wanted to do this room myself, since this is where the fire started."

"And you haven't started yet." Keith said it more like a statement than a question.

"No. I guess I was keeping it around like a reminder."

Garrison turned completely around to look at Malcolm. "You needed a burnt room to remind you not to fall asleep with a cigarette in your hand while drunk."

Keith picked up a sledgehammer and without looking at anyone in particular said, "What's that thing Fat Albert used to say all the time?"

"No class," Malcolm reminded him.

"That's right."

"What?" G. looked between his two friends.

Keith threw his jacket to the side. "Come on. Let's get to work. This is going to take a while."

Malcolm shook his head. "Not that long. I just need y'all for demo. I'll do the rest myself."

***

When Morgana opened the door, Keith handed her the dozen red roses he'd picked up earlier that evening.

She opened the door wide and stepped aside.

"They're beautiful. Thank you." She buried her nose in the bouquet and inhaled deeply.

"You're welcome. I'm really sorry about last week. I thought we were on the same page."

She ushered him into the kitchen where she looked for a vase. "No worries. It was just a misunderstanding. Anyone could have forgotten the address."

Keith stopped. "I didn't forget the address."

"Yes, you did. You said the restaurant was on Piedmont, downtown."

"That restaurant is downtown."

"No, it's uptown. Which is why I was forty minutes late getting back there and we missed our reservation."

He reached to massage the back of her neck. "Well, we made the best of it anyway, right?"

"Yes, the pizza and downloaded movie were very nice."

He nodded. "And tonight will be even nicer."

"Good." She reached for her jacket. "You have the directions?"

"Already plugged into the GPS. And you made the reservations, right?"

Morgana stopped, mid-step. "I thought you were supposed to take care of everything."

"Why would you think that?"

She took a deep breath. "Because you said 'I'll take care of everything.'"

Keith was confused. "But I asked you where we were going."

She nodded automatically. "Right. And I told you, the little Caribbean spot on the edge of the city.

"Was I supposed to know what that was?"

She was trying her best to stay calm. "Well, you didn't say you didn't know, in fact, all I recall you saying is 'I'll take care of everything.' "

He checked his watch. "Maybe they'll accept us without reservations?"

She slumped into her chair in defeat. "No, you absolutely need reservations to get into that place."

He ran his hand over his head and watched her become more withdrawn. "Chinese?"

She blew the curl that had fallen into her eyes and stood to get the remote from the other side of the room. "I'll check the movie guide."

***

Trent turned the stove down to simmer and looked over at Raegan. "You know, we have time for a quickie before dinner."

Raegan held the large wooden spoon between them. "No. You know I promised the girls I'd stick to this celibacy pact. We're supposed to be communicating remember?"

He held both hands out, in front of him. "I was

trying to communicate."

She blew out a frustrated breath. "Talking. Come on, tell me something I should know about you."

"Um, okay. I really want to have sex right now."

"You know, I'm starting to think you're addicted. We have the rest of our lives to have sex."

"Okay, but what if, God forbid, one of our lives ends early."

Raegan set the spoon down and pondered his words. "Well, I guess these things do happen. One moment you're here and the next minute you're on your deathbed. I do see what you're saying."

He nodded. "Exactly."

She smiled demurely before turning back to the stove. "Sweetie, for the record, if the last thoughts before you die are about how I didn't give you enough sex, then I'm in the wrong relationship and you need to let me know now, so I can move on."

"Whoa. What?"

"You heard me. If the only reason you're with me is to have sex, then you should let me know and I..."

He put up his hand to stop the tirade he knew was about to erupt.

"Stop. I'm with you because I love you and because you've been there for me, as one of my best friends, for the last twenty years. We're good together and the sex is great. I'm not about to give that up."

She pulled back to look in his eyes. "Then why were you pushing the sex thing so hard tonight?"

Trent took a deep breath, cleared his throat, stepped back and got down on one knee. "I was trying to set a romantic atmosphere but you just jacked that up."

"Oh!" Her hands flew up to her face.

He pulled the ring out of his pocket with a laugh. "Raegan, will you make me the happiest man on earth and become my wife?"

"Yes!"

***

Garrison leaned back on his headboard and put the phone up to his ear. The call had just connected but went straight into voice mail. "Hey Abril, it's G., I got your message last night but I was crazy busy at work. Looks like we're back to phone tag. Call me later. All right, bye."

He hung up and shook his head. He and Abril had barely even talked. Not that he could blame her. He knew she still had a thing for Malcolm. Truth be told, he would have liked to end up with Imani, if she wasn't so... so... He thought about it. Yes, she was loud, even inappropriate at times, but she knew him well enough to offer the correct advice in almost every situation. He heard her say that girl he'd just got a divorce from wasn't right for him, but he chose not to listen. That girl was a freak in bed and that's all he could think about. But deep down inside, he knew Imani was right.

That was why he avoided her and married his now ex-wife. He went over the situation in his mind over and over again until he came to a conclusion. It was time for a change. Malcolm still loved Abril and she still loved him. There was no need for he and Imani to step into the middle of that. He may as well do them all a favor.

He turned on his laptop and pulled up the video chat application. He hadn't used it in a while, but now was as good a time as any. He sent the invitation for a video chat and waited, hoping she hadn't gone to bed already.

Imani looked up from a book when her computer made a sound like a doorbell. *Who in the world is trying to chat at this time of night?*

She walked over to her desk and pulled up the video chat application. When she looked at the invite, her eyebrows shot up. What was Garrison doing reaching out to her after he had basically ignored her for the last few years?

"Garrison?"

"Yeah, you busy."

Her mind took a moment to catch up with what was going on. "Uh, no. Just getting ready to put this book down and go to bed. What's up?"

He shrugged. "Nothing. I just called to see how you and Malcolm were doing."

"Oh, we're fine."

G. was beyond surprised. "Really?"

Imani laughed and took his mind back to simpler times. "No. Not really. He's driving me crazy and not in a good way."

"Whew! I thought it was just me. Abril barely has time to talk, and when we do it's so... vague. I think she still has a thing for Malcolm."

Imani knew that to be true. "And I know he still has a thing for her. They belong together."

"Yeah, so why don't we make it easy for them?"

"Yeah, we should do that, it's just..."

He knew what she was about to say. "Hey, he's going to have to find out sooner or later. It's been too damn long already, if you ask me."

Imani sighed. "I guess you're right. I'll let her know tomorrow."

He was relieved. His plan was now in motion. "Okay, and I know it's late so I'll let you go, but I'll give you a call tomorrow evening."

Imani shook her head. "You don't have to do that. If we're not compatible, we don't need to force it."

He thought about not saying anything, but if things were really going to change, he would need to start sometime. "Look, I should have said something that night. I wanted to be with you but..."

"Why didn't you say something?"

"Because you were smacking your gum and rolling your neck, and..., because I'm an idiot. Forgive me?"

"I guess so."

"Good, what's the weather going to be doing in Birmingham this weekend?"

Imani checked her smart phone. "Cold and rainy."

A slow smile spread across Garrison's face. "Sounds like perfect weather for staying in. You good with company this weekend?"

"Yeah, I can do company this weekend."

***

Abril looked horrified. "Imani!" She was looking at her friend through her computer screen. "You know why I didn't want to be stuck with Malcolm."

"I know, sweetie." Imani tried to sympathize, but she couldn't handle another day of Malcolm. "And I'm sorry, but it couldn't be helped. I really can't take him any more."

Abril sighed. She should have known this was a bad idea to begin with. Imani and Malcolm would never have worked, not with their personalities being the way they were. "I understand. I know how he can be."

"Abs, don't you think it's time to face the truth?"

"Face it! I've been living with the truth for the last twenty years."

"That wasn't what I was talking about and you know it. You still love him."

"No." Abril's voice didn't waver. Her eyes, however, told a different story.

"Abril..."

"No. Whatever I felt for him died that night twenty years ago."

Imani leaned in closer to her laptop and stared Abril in the eyes. "Really? Because I think you suppressed it, and understandably because he acted like an ass, but I'm thinking it's still there. But that's not what I called to tell you."

Abril grew worried at the tone of Imani's voice and the look on her face. "What do you mean?"

"Well, when I told Malcolm I was switching to G., he didn't take it well."

"You mean he got upset?"

Imani shook her head. "No, just the opposite in fact."

Abril was confused. "I don't understand."

"He was happy, hell, he was almost ecstatic."

"But…"

"Abby, he was happy because that meant he could now pursue you with no obstacles in his way. He still loves you."

"No, that's not right. That can't be."

"It absolutely is. Which is why I called to warn you."

"Warn me about what?"

"He's coming to Denver this weekend."

"What?" Abril almost came out of her chair.

Imani nodded her confirmation. "He didn't want me to tell you, but I knew you'd freak out."

"Oh, no. Oh, God, what am I going to do?"

Imani tried to calm her friend down. "Abby, it's time. You can do this."

"No I can't. I won't."

"Abril! You can and you will, now get a hold of yourself. You've got three days. Tomorrow you can clear out all the pictures."

"No."

"The day after that, you deal with Jade's bedroom."

"Unh-unh. It's not going to work."

"You just said last month that you wanted to turn it into an office. You can get your stuff out of the living room and into a real space designated as an office."

Abril began to massage her temples. "I've got a headache."

"The day after that you go to an all-day spa and get gorgeous to let his crazy ass know what he's been missing."

"That's the only part of your plan that I like."

"Abril, you still love him and he loves you. It's time to end all the secrecy."

Abril placed a palm under her chin and thought over the situation. "I guess you're right. I knew it was going to happen one day."

Imani nodded again. "Yes, it's time. But you can do this. Just stick to the plan and act surprised when he shows up."

"Right. Stick to the plan. I can do that."

***

Abril sat nervously in the living room of her townhome. It was nowhere as big as Malcolm's house, but she had done all right for herself and Jade. It was nicely decorated and well maintained. The money she had made from her travel business had allowed for a descent living. It also enabled her to send some money to Jade while she was in college. It wasn't a lot of money, but it didn't need to be. Jade had earned a full scholarship.

Abril wondered what Malcolm would think of his brilliant daughter. Would he be proud or nonchalant? Not that she was going to find out tonight. She could admit that things worked out like they did for a reason. It was the universe's way of telling her that she needed to let Malcolm know he had produced a child almost twenty years ago. And she would, as soon as she made sure he was ready.

If this was the old Malcolm about to show up at her door, she wouldn't have to worry much. He would just ignore it and pretend like Jade didn't exist. If, however, he had started to turn his life around like the others suggested, she would have to think about that. How do you let someone who destroyed everything back into your life? What if he really wanted to be a part of Jade's life? What if Imani was right and he really wanted to be a part of her life again? She wasn't able think on it any longer because the doorbell rang.

On her way to the door, she noticed a small picture of herself with Jade on the mantle. She stuffed it into her pocket and continued moving toward the door. She took a deep breath and reminded herself that she was supposed to act surprised. She opened the door and tried to give her best "surprised" face.

"Malcolm? What are you doing here?"

"You look great."

"Thanks, but what are you doing here?"

"Imani kicked me to the curb for G."

"Oh." She wasn't sure what to say or do next.

Malcolm, on the other hand, was totally comfortable. "Yeah, I tried to call you after the reunion. By the way, it's kind of cold out. Do you mind if I come in?"

"Oh, sorry. Come on in."

"Thanks." He took his coat off and hung it on the coat rack by the door. "But, like I said, I tried to reach you awhile back."

"I must have been busy."

"Right. This is a nice place you have here." He looked around the home and noticed that it had what his house was missing. It felt like a real home. "I wasn't interrupting anything was I?"

"No." Abril shook her head. "Would you like something to drink?"

"Um, yeah. Whatever you've got is fine."

Abril left him in the living room and headed for the kitchen. She could barely breathe, much less think. It seemed so surreal that he was even here. Twenty years of no contact and he just strolls in like they never stopped talking.

She pulled the coffeemaker out and plugged it in. "You can do this. Just stick to the plan." She was so busy talking to herself that she didn't hear Malcolm walk up behind her.

"Hey, Abril?"

She spun around. "Yes?"

"Look, I know things haven't been right between us for awhile, and I'm sorry about that because I'm not exactly sure what I did wrong."

"You're not exactly sure…"

He took a few more steps into the kitchen. "Can we just let the past be the past and move forward? We can even start fresh if you like. However you want to do it."

She studied him quietly for a bit. "Okay." *New Malcolm it is.*

Chapter 7

Jade stuffed chocolate cake in her mouth between bites of chicken noodle soup like she would never eat again. She had set her textbooks off to the side in order to keep them free of crumbs and stains.

"What, no pickles and ice cream?" Callie smiled at her friend.

"I actually had some ice cream a few days ago. I think the baby's lactose intolerant. Feels like I've been on a roller coaster the last few days. So no dairy for a while."

"All right." Callie slung her backpack over her shoulder and reached for her keys. "I'm headed over to Jordan's place for the weekend. You gonna be all right?"

"Go. I'm fine. I'll call someone if I need anything."

"Are you sure? Your baby bump is getting bigger by the minute."

"Yeah, I can do this. My mom had me early, and I'll manage just like she did."

"I know you'll be fine." Callie had come to think of Jade as a sister. "I just hate to leave you."

"Go." Jade waved her off. "And tell Jordan hello for me. He really is a good guy."

Callie grinned. "I know. I think I'll keep him. Please call me if you need to, okay? I can be back over here in twenty minutes."

"I will."

"Did you tell your mom yet?"

Jade shook her head. "No. I think it will be easier if I just show up with her beautiful grandchild in my arms. She's less likely to go crazy that way."

Callie looked unsure. "Okay, if you think that's best. Don't forget to call me if you need to."

"I promise, now go. A good man is hard to find. You don't want to keep him waiting."

***

Garrison pulled up to Imani's house at seven o'clock on Friday evening. He was finally going to get what he wanted. Twenty years ago he had spotted Imani standing outside the student union center. He wanted to approach her then, but didn't. A few weeks later when they finally met, she was seeing someone else. He started seeing someone else soon after, and they just remained friends.

She could always read him like a book, though. That's part of the reason he ran for so long. Being around someone who knew you that well could be unnerving. Her mouth didn't help matters. Her tongue was sharp, too sharp sometimes but he could handle it. At least he hoped he could. *God help me.*

A few minutes later he stood at the door with a picnic basket in hand. He'd packed it with food right before he left Atlanta. She answered the door and stood aside to let him in, but he noticed that she was quiet. Imani had never been quiet for as long as he'd known her. He didn't know how to handle a quiet

Imani. He came in and looked around wondering if everything was all right. When she still hadn't said anything, he set the picnic basket down and stared at her.

She locked the door and finally turned to face him. "How was the drive from Atlanta?"

He smiled. "Traffic was crazy. I brought dinner."

"Thanks. That was nice of you. We can spread out in front of the fireplace."

"That sounds good." At least she was talking, but she was so subdued.

Imani walked toward the stairs to grab a blanket out of the closet. Garrison knew he would have to create a better atmosphere if he was going to get anywhere with her this weekend. He walked up behind her and waited for her to close the closet door and turn around.

"Oh!" She tried to take a step back but there was nowhere to go.

"Hey, Mani?"

"Yeah?"

"I missed you." He said it quietly then kissed her senseless.

"Oh, my." This was the Garrison she knew and remembered, the charmer and funny guy who had a way of getting under your skin. "I missed you, too. I'm glad it worked out the way it did." She was speaking in a near whisper and didn't realize it was driving him crazy. "Abril and Malcolm belong together, and it's finally happening."

"So, I guess by default, that means you and me belong together, too. Right?"

She looked up into his eyes and smiled. "I'll let you know in a couple of months."

He kissed her again, but he took his time and persisted until he felt her start to melt under the soft pressure. When he was sure that she was completely pliable, he pulled back and looked into her eyes. "Why so long?"

***

Morgana touched the corners of her mouth with the cloth napkin that Keith laid out with dinner. They'd finally made it to a restaurant last month, only to discover that they preferred quiet nights at home with just the two of them.

"Mmm, that was so good. Where did you learn to cook like that?"

Keith stood up and extended his hand. He watched as she grabbed it and then pulled her upright. "My mom made sure all of us knew how to cook before we left the house." He guided her into the living room and sat down with her on the sofa. "She didn't want to leave our stomachs in the hands of some hapless female."

She turned slightly and leaned against him. "Smart woman. Thank her for me next time you see her."

He let his hand wander up to her hair and stroked it. "You could just thank her yourself at the next family reunion."

Morgana turned around to face him. Her eyes had grown to the size of small saucers. "Are you asking me to your family reunion?"

Keith reached out for her hand. "Well, we've spent countless hours on the phone, and every evening together for the last few months, so I figured the next step was to meet the families."

"Wow, that's pretty serious. I mean you're asking me to meet your entire family."

Keith slid down on one knee and pulled out a ring. "Actually, I'm asking a lot more than that."

"Oh!" Her hands flew to her mouth.

"Morgana Witherspoon, I know I've known you for over twenty years but I have completely fallen in love with you over the last few months. Will you do me the honor of becoming my wife?"

Morgana didn't mean to go into the ugly cry, but she couldn't help herself. She was completely overwhelmed. She had waited so long and here was her knight in shining armor before her, asking for her hand in marriage. She lost complete control of her faculties. "I...I..."

"Morgana? I'm not alone here am I? I thought you were..."

"No." She shook her head emphatically.

"O...kay." Keith stood and put the ring back in his pocket.

Her tears stopped immediately. "Wait, what are you doing?"

"You just said you didn't want to marry me."

"I said nothing of the sort."

"You just said 'no'." He looked at her like she'd gone mad.

"Because you just asked if you were alone in what you were feeling."

"But you didn't answer my question."

Morgana jumped up. "Can I have a minute to enjoy the moment? I mean it takes you twenty years to ask the question and you want the answer in point five seconds?"

He stood to join her. "Um... so do you want to marry me?"

She put both hands on either hip and looked up at Keith. "I should be asking you the same thing. You put that ring up mighty fast, like you had somewhere you needed to be."

He kissed her quickly before she had time to say anything else, and made sure that when they pulled apart, the kiss was the only thing on her mind.

"All better?"

She smiled happily. "Yes."

"Good. Will you marry me?"

"Yes." She watched as he slipped the ring on her finger then pulled her hand up to his lips for a kiss.

"I love you, Keith."

"I love you too, baby."

***

Quentin laughed heartily. "I knew it. I knew they still had a thing for each other."

Stacia shifted the phone as she lay back in bed. "Well, we all knew Malcolm and Abril still had a thing for each other. That was never the issue. I just hope they aren't building up a relationship that's doomed to fall apart in the end."

"Hmm. You think she'll tell him about Jade soon?"

Stacia shrugged her slim shoulders. "Hard to say. I think she's definitely ready to stop carrying around the secret. But you know Malcolm and his temper. What's going to happen when he finds out he has a daughter in college and that we've all known for twenty years but never told him?"

"Yeah, I thought about that. I also wonder how Jade's going to react. I mean, that guy Bryan was the only father she's ever known. How's she going to handle it when she finds out that Abril, and all of her aunts and uncles have been keeping the truth from her for all of her life?"

She sighed, heavily. "I know. It's a big mess. But it's not like you can blame Abril. I wouldn't have told Malcolm anything either. Up until five years ago, he was a complete mess and a functioning alcoholic. I wouldn't have allowed him anywhere near my child either, even if he was the father. A barely sober man does not make a good father in any way, shape, or form."

Quentin agreed, but things were different now. "Yeah, but now that he's got himself together, he'll hopefully be able to understand her reasoning when it comes time to tell him. But enough about Malcolm. When are you coming to Chicago?"

"Nice try." Stacia smiled as she said it. "But as you well know, I just left Chicago. So when are you coming to Vegas?"

"Can't blame a guy for trying, and don't kill me but something came up at work today and I won't be able to make it down for another five or six weeks, at least."

"Five or six weeks!" Stacia sat straight up in bed. "Honey, come on. We've got a guest list to pare down and your mom sent more names today."

"I know, baby. I'm sorry, but you know how it is when you run your own business."

112

She leaned back into her pillows, disappointment written all over her face. "I know. Everything falls on you."

"Yes. And starting next week, I'm going to be on the road for a while."

"Fine, but you better call."

"Everyday."

***

Quentin called the meeting to order by banging the tongs from the hotel ice bucket on the small desk in the room. He and the guys got together over video chat about two or three times a year, just to catch up with each other. He'd been traveling for four weeks straight, but he took time out to meet like this whenever he could.

"All right gentlemen, this meeting is now in session. So... what's up?"

Garrison was the first to answer. "Nothing man, all is good in my world since Malcolm hooked up with the right woman."

"Yeah. Mine, too. " Malcolm couldn't help but smile. "But what we really want to know is, how are the wedding plans coming for big brother Q?"

Quentin smiled back at his friends. "Aw man, it's crazy- the band, the caterers, the guest list. It's an absolute mad house, but I wouldn't change anything for the world."

Trent shook his head. "Man, you're better than me. This stuff is starting to drive me crazy and I'm not lovin' it. I'm seriously considering eloping."

"Eloping is good. That's what we did." Every one stopped what they were doing to focus on Garrison. No one said anything for a time.

"What!" Quentin moved closer to his laptop screen to get a good look at his friend's face. Garrison was always known for his jokes, but he wasn't smiling this time.

"When?" Trent wanted to know.

"Last weekend." Garrison shrugged his shoulders with palms extended upward. "Hey. We're old and not trying to go through that whole wedding thing again, but Quentin and Trent, good luck with that."

Trent was still in disbelief. "You mean to tell me that you and Imani are already married?"

Garrison nodded. "Afraid so, man. We rolled through the JP last weekend. I moved to Birmingham until she sells the house, then she's back in the ATL."

Malcolm looked downright uncomfortable. Commitment wasn't his forte but some of his friends apparently had no problem with it.

"Uh, guys?" Keith who had been quiet up until that point cleared his throat. "Morgana and I did the same thing. We got married last weekend too."

"Dayum! Y'all starting to make a brother feel downright slow." Malcolm pretended to pat his brow dry, and was only partly joking.

Trent agreed. "I'm saying. I'ma see if Rae will go for the low-budget version."

Quentin knew better than to ask. "I know Stacia wouldn't hear of it but I'm good with that. So congratulations to Garrison and Trent. Anybody else got anything they want to share. You don't have kids on the way do you?"

Keith cleared his throat again. "Well.. er..uh."

"No." Quentin said the word to Keith like he wouldn't allow it.

Malcolm wasn't as restrained. "Oh, hell no!"

"Easy fellas." Keith just laughed at their reaction. "We're just looking at adoption agencies. Relax."

Garrison released his heart and chuckled. "Whew, bruh, you had me worried for a minute."

"Uh, G., you laughing, but you sure you ain't expecting any?" Trent knew his friend was full of surprises.

He denied it, however. "Nah, man. We just had that conversation a few days ago. We're child-free at the moment."

"Good. Stay that way and let the rest of us catch up with you two." Hearing them talk about their marriages so casually actually put Malcolm at ease. He could now see himself married to Abril... sometime in the future.

Keith pointed at his computer screen. "Hey, this is all Quentin's fault. He's the one that stood up making speeches about dying alone and stuff."

Quentin smiled. "Yeah. My bad. But everyone's good, right?"

Garrison returned the good will. "Yeah, bruh. We're good."

***

Imani put her feet up on the sofa and waited for Garrison to turn on the television. He joined her moments later and placed her feet in his lap.

"I talked to the guys the other day and told them we got married."

She drew her attention away from screen and focused on her husband. "Yeah. I know. I've been getting calls all week from the girls.

"So you know about Keith and Morgana?"

She nodded. "Yeah. We had a good long talk."

"Did she tell you they were looking at adoption agencies?"

"No. That didn't come up. That's interesting."

"Yeah." He agreed. "I talked to Keith yesterday and they're thinking about slightly older kids, maybe a sibling group."

"More power to them for doing that. I love the idea of older kids, but dealing with someone else's kids is something else. I need to catch those jokers from birth. You're missing time to train them when you let them go past three years. No. No older kids."

He stopped what he was doing to look at her. "So, that's it. I don't get to weigh in on the decision?"

"Of course you can, baby. Are you going to handle all the craziness that comes with adopting older kids?"

"I can, just like Keith and Morgana are doing."

Imani batted her eyes sweetly, then filled her voice with sugar. "But honey, my name is not Morgana." She took a deep breath and tried with everything in her to keep calm. "My name is Imani, and if you want to handle it by yourself, then you go right ahead. Just make sure your bank account stays healthy."

"For what?"

"For bail money, because I don't have a problem killing somebody! You just make sure you keep that in mind while you're making decisions."

116

"And you need to keep in mind that we are now married."

"And?" Her body language screamed with defiance.

"And I don't have a problem discussing issues that come up, but we will absolutely not be letting Imani's temper tantrums make decisions in our marriage. Got it?"

She was taken aback, but more than a little impressed. He was always so easy-going. It was nice to know he wouldn't allow himself to be walked on, albeit a little frustrating at the moment.

"Fine."

***

Stacia looked at the stack of papers in front of her and shook her head. "This is quickly getting out of hand. We're at three-hundred people already and we haven't even gotten to the names our parents sent us."

Quentin looked over her shoulder. "You sure you can't drop a couple of tables? I mean how often do you see your third cousins, twice removed?"

Stacia picked up the seating chart and looked it over. "Oh, you want me to drop some people? Okay, let's see. I'll drop the cousins if you drop Aunt Bertha and Uncle Frank's tables."

Quentin's eyebrows drew together. "I can't drop them. They're family."

"So are my cousins," she countered.

"Fine. Keep the cousins but we don't need to spend $100,000 on one day out of the rest of our lives. We are not getting any younger and we need to keep our nest egg in tact."

"Maybe we can have the wedding in Malcolm's backyard. That would save a few bucks"

He looked pleasantly surprised. "More than a few. Now, there's a good idea. It's definitely big enough."

"Yeah," she smiled cunningly. "Or we could have it at The Little White Wedding Chapel, which just happens to be right up the road from my house. We could be married by dinner and planning our less expensive reception by dessert."

"Stacia, don't tempt me. I was doing this to make you happy."

She stood up to wrap her arms around him. "Aww, sweetie, I'm already happy. I don't need an over-the-top wedding for you to prove that you love me."

Quentin kissed her quickly. "Okay, let's go."

"What? Where? Now?"

"Weren't you the one that just said we could be married by dinner?"

"That was a figure of speech. We can't go right now. There are still things we need to discuss."

"Like what?"

She wrung her hands nervously. "Like, we live in two different states."

He shrugged. "So, we can pack up your stuff over the weekend and have it shipped up to Chicago. What's the problem?"

"The problem is, I never agreed to move to Chicago."

He was dumbfounded. "So, we were just going to live in two separate states for the rest of our lives?"

"You never even considered moving to Nevada, did you? It's all about you, huh?" She crossed her arms over her chest in a huff.

"Outside of that four year stint for school, I've lived in Chicago my whole life." He rubbed the back of his neck trying to ease the tension away then turned and walked out of the room.

Stacia watched him go but couldn't believe it. "Great."

Quentin came back into the room seconds later with keys in hand. "Come on, let's go."

"Go where?"

"Where do you think?"

"But we haven't..."

"We're going to dinner Stacia. We need to talk, and I'm going to need food in front of me because I can see this is going to be a long conversation."

***

Abril dropped the grocery bags on the kitchen counter before walking over to the answering machine. She smiled as Jade's voice came through.

"Hey, mama. I didn't want anything. Just wanted to see what you had planned for the rest of this week. All right, well, I'll talk to you later. Love you. Bye."

Abril shook her head and began putting groceries away. "What am I doing this weekend? Oh, nothing much, talking to your aunts and then spending the weekend with your father, whom you've never met."

***

Trent and Raegan stood looking up at the Las Vegas Wedding Chapel, preparing to go in.

He shifted his eyes away from the chapel and on to her. "Are you sure you're okay with this? Just say the word and the big, expensive, time-consuming wedding is back on."

Raegan laughed. "Are you kidding me? You shaved ten years off my life with this move. If I had to sit down with that crazy wedding planner one more time, I was going to lose it. As long as we still do the reception, I'm more than okay."

"Well, come on soon-to-be Mrs. Trent McAllister, let's get this party started."

***

Stacia made sure all the ladies had called in for their monthly conference call. They'd decided to keep in touch more at the previous reunion.

"Good evening ladies. How's everyone?"

Imani answered for all the women. "We're good."

Stacia couldn't hold back her laughter. "Most of you should be since you're married now."

Morgana laughed with her friend. "Oh, come on now, don't act like you didn't start this. Seven and a half months ago we were all single, and just fine with our single status."

Stacia couldn't deny that. "Yeah, I guess I had a hand in it. And it looks like I've created some monsters."

"Happy monsters. What's going on with your wedding plans?" Raegan's voice broke in.

"Oh, it's no longer a wedding. It's turned into a complete three-ring circus. But it's fine. Y'all need to send me measurements for your bridesmaid's dresses soon."

"Abril, honey, what's been going on with you? I haven't heard a lot from you recently." Morgana sounded concerned.

"Uh, maybe because you're still in the honeymoon phase of your relationship and paying no attention to anybody else."

"Well, that may be partially true." Morgana said. "But, you have been awfully quiet the last few months. How's it going with Malcolm?"

"Actually, It's better than I could have expected. He's been flying up every weekend and acting like a real gentleman." Abril almost couldn't believe how well it was going.

Imani's eyebrows rose in surprise. "Wow, I'm impressed. Did you...? You know."

"Tell him about Jade yet? No." Abril shook her head. "But, since things have been going so well, I thought I'd do it this weekend. He's coming up tomorrow."

Imani was happy that all her friends were happy, but especially happy that Abril was working things out with Malcolm. "Good. And, Stacia, you may want to hold off on those measurements because pregnancy is a trip!"

"AH! Imani you are not pregnant!"

"Pregnant? No, but this surrogate is having major discomfort!"

"Surrogate!" Raegan balked. "If a surrogate is having your baby, what's the weight gain have to do with you?"

"I'm having sympathy cravings and they are no joke, I've already gained ten pounds!"

Chapter 8

Abril opened the door to her home and allowed Malcolm to enter. She held out her hand for his coat, thinking they would have a nice cozy evening in, but he shook his head.

"Grab your coat, let's go."

She was truly astounded. "Where are we going?"

"It's a surprise. Now come on, move it. And hand over your cell phone. I don't want any interruptions tonight."

Abril pulled her phone out reluctantly.

"I don't know about that."

She was rarely without it, but she did say that she was going to be more open to new things, especially with Malcolm coming back into her life. He snatched the phone out of her hand and stuffed it into his pocket.

"Come on. You can talk to your nosy friends tomorrow."

She grinned with satisfaction. "I've already talked to them this week."

"That's nice, but just in case, I don't want anyone cutting in on my time."

"Fine."

Malcolm ushered Abril to his rental car. After she was seated he pulled onto the highway and then a remote road. They'd been driving for quite a while but Malcolm kept her entertained with memories from long ago.

"Hey, I was home free." Malcolm laughed loudly.

Abril joined him in the mirth. "Until Dean Starks realized it was you holding the freshly decapitated cement head of one of the school's founding fathers."

"All that evidence was circumstantial. And the charges were trumped up."

"Is that why they found a hack saw and drill under your mattress?"

"Cheap ass school. If we had real mattresses they wouldn't have been able to make out the big lump in the middle of the bed."

She smiled. "You are still crazy. How far away is this place, anyway? We've been driving for like forty minutes."

Abril was enjoying herself immensely, more than she ever thought possible. She was beginning to feel like herself, like her old self, once again. She was sure she would tell him about Jade this weekend. They didn't have much time before he left, but she wanted to enjoy this side of Malcolm for a little while longer. It was like she was getting pay back for all those years ago. *Maybe I'll tell him tomorrow.*

He wheeled the car into a dimly lit lot and brought it to a stop between faintly painted lines. "I have no idea what you're talking about because we're already here."

"Ohh," she gasped.

124

"You remember?"

She grinned fondly. "Of course I do. You brought me here sophomore year when you drove up for a week that summer."

He rushed out and around the car to open her door. "Yeah, I thought it'd be nice to visit it again. With you."

"Thanks. That was very thoughtful of you."

"I'm a thoughtful kind of guy."

"When you want to be." She nodded.

They enjoyed a quiet dinner, reminiscing about the past and getting reacquainted. He'd essentially been walking on eggshells with her the last couple of months. Based on her initial reaction, he hadn't wanted to press her too much, so he usually kept the conversation light. But because she seemed more relaxed tonight, he thought he would go further. They were halfway through their dinner when he steered the conversation into more personal territory. "So how are your parents doing?"

She stared across the restaurant with a vacant look. "They passed away several years ago."

"Wow, I'm sorry. I didn't know. Do you mind telling me about it?"

She sighed. "Not much to tell, really. They were on their way home from an Anita Baker concert the fall of our senior year when a drunk driver slammed into their car. Mom died instantly and Daddy made it to the hospital but couldn't hold on long. He died before I reached home."

He saw that the memory still stirred up pain, and reached for her hand to offer comfort.

"I'm sorry, sweetie, I know how that feels. The same thing happened to my parents."

She looked at him with her mouth open. "I don't think I knew that."

"I've never told anyone else." That was one of the reasons that he never got behind the wheel when he drank. "Granny is the only other soul on the planet, besides you, who knows. But still, I was really young. That must have been hard on you, especially at that age."

She thought of Jade and smiled. It was the birth of her infant daughter a couple of months later that helped her through that difficult time in her life. "It was, but God and time have a way of making things better. How's your Granny doing?"

"Oh, she's great. She still remembers you. I told her I was coming up this weekend and she asked me to tell you hello and give you a big hug."

Abril remembered the old woman affectionately. "She's so sweet. Is she still living by herself or does she need help to get around."

"No, she doesn't need any help. In fact, she fusses at me every time I try to bring it up. I can't even drop off a few groceries without getting the riot act."

"She wants to remain independent. That's a good thing."

Malcolm was undecided. "Yeah, I guess so. She moves slower than she used to, though, so I try to get by there more often now."

"Tell her I said hello next time you talk to her."

He swallowed a gulp of iced tea. "I'll do that. So now tell me about you. I know you've been in the travel industry since we left school and I'm trying to figure out how that happened since you studied world languages and literature for four years."

She smiled wryly. "Yeah, well there weren't many language and literature jobs available when I graduated and I needed to eat so I took a job at a travel agency." She thought back to that time and remembered how stressful it was with an infant daughter and no parents to help her. Her aunt was her only saving grace. She helped Abril out until she could get on her feet with the baby. It was stressful, but she managed with her aunt's help and a lot of prayer. "It hasn't been all bad though. I opened my own company a while back and I've been doing all right. So tell me about you, investment banker extraordinaire."

One corner of his mouth lifted humbly. "I wouldn't go that far."

Abril swallowed the last of her steak before she dabbed the corners of her mouth. "I think the size of your house disagrees with you."

"No, I just lucked up and got with a good company right after graduation. Thankfully, the bosses liked me and I kept getting promotions. I just celebrated twenty years with them."

"That's really great. I'm happy for you." And she was. She could honestly say that she was truly happy about the way things turned out. It had been a little rough in the beginning, but she made it and she had nothing but gratitude for the experiences she had along the way.

"Thank you, but I'd like to propose a toast." He raised his glass and waited until she did the same.

She brought her glass within centimeters of his. "What we are drinking to?"

"Here's to new beginnings."

***

Quentin used a pairing knife to chop the celery for the gumbo and threw it into the pot. He stirred it before tasting a sample.

"Hmm. I think it's missing something."

Stacia dipped her finger in the pot and tasted it also. "Really? What's it missing?"

"I think it needs a little sugar."

"You know, that's funny." Stacia put down the large spoon in her hand. "I was just thinking that I could use some sugar, myself."

"Were you now? Because, strangely enough, I was thinking the same thing."

She took off her apron next. "Well then, I guess we better take care of that before something awful happens."

Quentin reached for her, but stopped his hands, midway. "Wait, you're still...?"

"Celibate? Yes," she confirmed. After only a second's hesitation, she offered another option. "But we could make out."

Quentin smiled and took hold of her waist before walking backward out of the kitchen. "Like, third base, make out?"

"Um, maybe second. I don't want to start anything I can't finish." The look in her eyes let him know she was serious.

"How far did you say that little wedding chapel is from here?"

***

Trent toweled himself dry from his recent dip in the pool and joined Raegan on the lounge chair next to hers. They'd picked the Bellagio Hotel as the place to spend their honeymoon, and had enjoyed it thoroughly. They'd be leaving in a couple of days and Trent, especially, didn't want to see it end. Raegan felt guilty because they hadn't let Stacia know they were in town, but Trent only laughed. "You think she's going to be thinking about us when she's on her honeymoon with Quentin? She'll understand."

Raegan watched lovingly as he walked away from the pool and over to her. She didn't say anything when he came to stand next her, just smiled.

"And how are you doing this evening, Mrs. McAllister?"

"I'm glad you asked, Mr. McAllister, because the truth is, I don't think I could get any happier."

He lay out on the empty lounge chair and closed his eyes. "That puts a smile on my face."

"Why?" She laughed. "Because you think you had something to do with it?"

"I had better have something to do with it."

She gave him a slight nod, begrudgingly. "Yeah, I guess you did."

"Don't play with me woman, not after you screamed my name like you did this morning."

Raegan laughed lightly. "Okay, you got me. You kinda rocked my world this morning."

Trent slowly raised himself off the lounge chair by his elbows to look at her. "Kinda? And this morning?"

"All right, sheesh. You rocked it out, all week, and almost too well."

"What do you mean almost too well?"

"Well, think about it. You show everything up front and you've got nothing to work with later. I mean, how do you plan on topping that?"

He huffed out a breath and sat up. The look on his face left no room for doubt about what he was thinking. She jumped up just in time, just before he grabbed her. She screamed and laughed her way back up to their suite with him following closely behind.

***

Keith and Morgana sat cuddled up on the sofa. They'd spent the last two hours reviewing the case files of older children waiting to be adopted. Many of them had spent most of their short lives in the foster care system and had never known a forever family.

Keith rubbed his eyes and leaned back. "Okay, what are we down to?"

Morgana stood up and stretched before returning to her seat. "We've got two sets left. This one is a group of four, three boys and one girl."

Keith shook his head. "There are so many kids out there."

"I know. I wish we could take them all."

He smiled every time he thought about how big her heart was. "Me, too. But I don't want to break our marriage up before we get started. Four is a lot to handle, especially when we're just starting out. What about the last set?"

Morgana opened the folder and gasped. "Oh, look at these two faces."

Keith looked at the picture. "Tell me about them."

"Mark was three when he was found wandering the streets. He told the police he was trying to find food for his baby sister. She was only a few months old at the time. They're eight and five now. They've been in four different homes already. Mark is starting to act out."

Her eyes continued to scroll down the page and Keith noticed a frown marring her lovely face.

"What's wrong?"

Her expression was a solemn one. "It looks like they're going to separate them on the next placement."

Keith considered the photo in his hand. "I can do eight and five. You?"

"Yeah, I'm good with eight and five. You know he's going to test you until he's sure you love him?"

He kissed her and pulled back to look in her eyes. "Baby, as long as I got you, I can handle anything that comes my way."

Morgana smiled brightly. "All right, then. Instant family, here we come."

***

Imani walked into the bedroom and joined Garrison on the bed.

"How is our favorite surrogate doing?"

She shrugged. "As well as can be expected, I suppose."

"Good."

"What did your son say when you told him we were expecting another child?"

"He was happy. Somebody else he can boss around."

She shook her head. "I'm glad I froze my eggs when I did. And I'm glad they implanted so well in our surrogate, but I don't know how women do that more than once. She looks so uncomfortable, like she's about to pop already."

He shook his head, in agreement with Imani "God bless her, 'cause it couldn't be me."

Imani laughed and swatted him playfully. "We should probably have the doctor check for more than one heart beat at the next visit."

"Excuse me?"

"Well he did implant more than one embryo."

He rubbed the back of his neck and shut his eyes. "We aren't going to get any sleep for the next few years, are we?"

She placed a hand on his chest in sympathy. "Probably not. So you know what that means."

"What?"

"We need to get it in now. Get to strippin'."

Garrison grabbed the remote control to the stereo and turned on the music. He began to shake and shimmy to the beat while slowly lifting his shirt over his head.

"Do it, Big Daddy!"

***

Malcolm pulled up in front of Abril's house and parked the car. He escorted her to the door and waited patiently. He knew it was going to take some time to win her back, but he figured he'd moved ahead several points tonight. He still couldn't figure out why she'd been so distant with him, but he was determined to get closer to her, no matter how long it took.

"Thank you, Malcolm. It was a lovely evening."

"You're welcome." When she didn't say anything he turned to leave with a promise that he would call once he reached his hotel room. He started down the walkway, but something stopped him. He turned and went back to stand in front of her.

"I have been wanting to kiss you all night. Do you mind?"

Abril shook her head slowly. "No, I don't mind."

She closed her eyes as he stepped forward to initiate the kiss. He applied just enough heat to make her soften and continued the assault until they were both breathless. Apparently, twenty years made no difference. Their bodies reacted to the kiss like they had never been apart. When she reached up to encircle his neck, he almost lost it. After pulling back and taking a moment to catch his breath, Malcolm placed his hands on either side of her face. He kissed her forehead, her nose and her lips once more.

"Good night, my lady."

"Good night."

"Go ahead inside. I'll wait here until I hear the door lock behind you."

She nodded. "Am I going to see you tomorrow?"

"You absolutely will. I've got another surprise planned for tomorrow."

She smiled back at him. "Good. I've kind of got a surprise for you, too."

"That sounds intriguing."

"It is, but we'll talk about it tomorrow. Sleep well."

"You too, baby. I'll call you when I get to the hotel."

He made sure she was inside the house before he headed back to the car. He had just started to put the car in reverse when he remembered that he had her phone. He was standing at her door a moment later. She looked surprised when she saw him standing there.

"Almost forgot to give you your phone back." He pulled the phone out and looked down. "Somebody named Jade has been blowing your phone up all night.."

"Oh, no!" She snatched the phone and began to dial the numbers frantically. She walked inside and Malcolm followed her out of concern.

"Honey, what's wrong?"

She never answered him. Abril checked the messages and sank down the wall that was holding her up.

Malcolm shut the door and took a step closer to Abril. "Baby?"

"She won't answer."

"Who won't? Who's Jade, sweetie?"

Abril was frantic and in a different world by this point. She checked her phone and found the number for Jade's roommate. She waited through several rings and someone picked up a short while later. "Yes! Hello? Who is this?... Callie, this is Ms. Barnes. What happened... Oh God.... Where are you? Okay. Okay. Calm down. No, I'll be there as soon as I can."

"What's wrong?" Malcolm had never seen her like this before. She looked as if she were about to lose her dinner.

She stood up in a daze and looked around the house. "I have to go."

"Where?" He tried to reach out for her, but she stepped back.

"I have to go."

"Baby, where do you need to go? I can take you."

"No, you can't. I have to go."

"Abril! You can't drive like this. Tell me where you need to go and I'll take you."

"The hospital."

"Okay, let's go."

Malcolm rushed her to the car and drove off quickly. Abril sat quietly and other than some tersely given directions, she didn't speak during most of the ride. Jade had picked a school that was in the state of Colorado, but it was a couple of hours away. Malcolm glanced over at Abril and noticed tears falling freely down her face. He covered her trembling hands with his free one.

"Honey, who is Jade?"

"My daughter."

He was shocked into silence. *Daughter?* How had he missed that? "I didn't know. I mean, I never saw..."

"She's in college."

"Oh." His thoughts immediately went to Bryan, and the last time he saw the other man at the reunion. He wanted to find Bryan right now and beat him to a pulp, but Abril's pain overshadowed everything else at the moment. His main focus was now getting her to Jade's hospital room.

Chapter 9

Malcolm had no sooner pulled up to the emergency entrance than Abril had the door open and was running inside. He parked the car and found his way to the information desk about ten minutes later. After he explained that he was with the woman who had just come in, they directed him to the elevators and he hopped in one, hoping to locate Abril quickly.

The floor he stepped out on was eerily quiet. There was no desk in sight, just a hallway of doors. He wandered around briefly until he spotted a young, college-aged woman pacing back and forth. He thought he'd approach her since there was no other option.

"Excuse me, I'm looking for Jade?"

Callie pointed to a door three feet away then walked away crying. He stepped into the room gingerly, not wanting to upset the atmosphere. He saw Abril on the far side of the bed, fawning over a young girl. He tried to be quiet as he entered, but they heard him. When the girl turned her head to look at him, he stopped breathing. Her eyes were the exact color of his grandmother's. The moment was over quickly because Jade turned back to Abril and continued their conversation. Malcolm noticed that she was weak. He could barely here her from where he stood, so he moved closer.

"I'm sorry, mama. I'm so sorry, mama."

Abril shushed her and dabbed a damp cloth on her forehead. "Shhh. Baby, there's nothing to be sorry about. Just save your strength."

Malcolm had reached them by the time Abril finished speaking, and Jade turned to face him once again. "Who's this?"

Abril took a deep breath and kept her eyes focused on Malcolm. God knows this wasn't the way she intended for either of them to find out. So much had happened in the last twenty years and neither one of them were aware of the role the other played in their lives. She saw the gravity of her mistake though, and she wanted to correct it before it was too late. She just hoped Malcolm had matured enough to set his feelings aside and focus on Jade.

Abril looked down at her daughter and prayed that she would understand. Jade had been crushed when Bryan left and had been seeking out a father figure ever since. Abril couldn't count how many times she'd had to deal with calls about Jade's inappropriate behavior with older men after Bryan left. She knew it was just a young girl's way of seeking out the affection that had been taken from her. Abril prayed that Malcolm's presence would make up for all of that in the future.

"I should have told you a long time ago that Bryan wasn't your father. This is your father, baby."

Malcolm froze in place. He eyed the girl, not with suspicion but with curiosity. He saw himself looking back, through his grandmother's eyes. If he were honest with himself, he knew she was his the moment he walked into the room and looked into her beautiful eyes. He honestly didn't know whether to jump up and down or throw something. All this time and this is how he finds out about a child he fathered decades ago. How could Abril keep this from him? He stared back at Abril, who was daring him, with her eyes to say anything out of line. He looked back at Jade and his anger dispersed. He would hold his tongue... for now.

Jade looked at Malcolm trying to make out if he would accept this new relationship, if he would accept her. She had dreamed of this forever and hoped he loved her as much as she loved him. "I knew Bryan wasn't my dad." Jade tried to reach her hand out to Malcolm, but didn't have the strength to complete the task. "You look like I thought you would."

Malcolm took her hand and held it tenderly. "You're beautiful, sweetheart. You have eyes like your great-grandmother."

Jade closed her eyes in relief. Tears began to flow from both father and daughter. "Thank you, Daddy. I didn't think I was ever going to hear you say that."

He leaned over and kissed her forehead. "I'll say it every day for the rest of your life."

She smiled feebly. "That shouldn't take too long."

Abril frowned. "Jade, don't say that. You're going to be fine."

"No, mom, I'm slipping. I can feel it. But it's all right. I'm ready to go."

Something rose up in Abril and she pulled out a voice she hadn't used on Jade since she was a little girl. "You are not. You are going to stay right here!"

"No, mom. I was just holding on so I could see you before I left and I got to see my dad too, so I'm happy. I'm just sorry I didn't listen to you. But I did pray like you taught me, so I'm ready to go."

"Jade, baby, please hold on." Abril said the words between sobs.

"I can't, mom. I'm so tired. I love you mom, and daddy too."

She smiled at them once more before she closed her eyes. They thought she'd fallen asleep until the heart monitor in the stark room beeped loudly. When they turned to look at it, all they saw was a continuous flat line.

"Doctor! Doctor!" Malcolm turned to run out of the room but the hospital staff was already coming in when he opened the door. He pulled Abril back, and they watched as the doctor and two nurses tried to resuscitate her. They worked on Jade for almost twenty minutes until they were sure she was gone.

Abril wept loudly against Malcolm. It was a long time before she quieted down. When she did, the doctor sat down before them with a solemn expression. "I'm so sorry... She lost a lot of blood in childbirth. If we'd gotten to her sooner..."

Malcolm shook his head. "I don't understand."

The doctor nodded and looked down at the chart in his hands. "She gave birth vaginally in her friend's bathtub. She was slightly premature, so no one suspected that she would be giving birth now. Her friends left her alone for several hours. The pregnancy was complicated. Your daughter didn't realize it, but she was bleeding internally."

"She was pregnant?"

"Yes. I'm so sorry. We didn't get the call until it was too late. She had already picked up the infection, and it multiplied quickly. If they had just been able to reach us a few hours earlier... I'm sorry. All we could really do was make her comfortable in the end."

Malcolm looked at Abril who was dazed. He felt the same way, like he was sleepwalking. He hoped to God this was a bad dream that he would wake up from soon. When Abril looked like she couldn't stand to be there a moment longer, he went into action.

"Thank you, doctor." Malcolm helped Abril stand and began to walk toward the elevators.

"Sir?"

"Yes?"

"I know we couldn't do much for your daughter, but we were able to treat your granddaughter. She should be ready to go home in a few days."

Abril turned around to look at the doctor. She was still numb and the words he spoke made no sense.

"Granddaughter?" Malcolm's voice echoed the blank expression on Abril's face.

The young doctor flipped through the chart once more. "Yes, sir. Jada Marie. We just need to make sure she didn't get exposed to the same infection that your daughter did, so we're going to keep her for a bit. I know it's been a long night. You two should go get some rest. You can come back and see her tomorrow. Visiting hours start at eleven."

***

Keith and Morgana were sound asleep. They both jumped up when the phone rang, but it was Morgana who grabbed it first.

"Hello... What? Oh no... Oh God."

Keith rubbed the sleep out of eyes and looked at his wife. He sat straight up when he saw the look on her face. "What is it? What happened?"

"It's Jade."

"Oh, God... Is she all right?"

Morgana shook her head and tried to wipe away the tears that had already formed. "No, she's gone."

"What!"

"She died in childbirth, but the baby is okay. We have to tell the others." She stood up and grabbed her robe off the chair. "Can you call the others? I'll make our flight and hotel arrangements now. Tell them to meet us there as soon as they can."

Keith turned on the light and found his phone. He started dialing as quickly as his fingers would allow.

***

Trent put Raegan's luggage in the overhead bin above their seats and sat next to her. Quentin did the same for Stacia and they waited for the plane to take off.

Trent looked across the aisle. "I spoke to all the guys. Everybody's good on the plan."

Raegan pulled a large planner out of her purse and looked over the to-do list. "Yes." She also looked across the aisle at their friends. "You two will go shopping for baby clothes, pampers and bottles."

Stacia nodded solemnly. "Right."

Trent grinned. "I'm sure, that little girl will be set for the next three years, with Stacia leading the way."

Quentin smiled at the attempt to make them laugh, but he knew Stacia could break down at any moment. He reached for her hand and tried to steady her nerves.

Raegan smiled. "You know it. Then Imani and Garrison are going to pick up the crib, bassinet, and changing table before they come to the house."

"Right." Quentin nodded. "Keith and Morgana are going to pick up the stroller, car seats, linens, and baby bags."

Raegan closed her planner. "And Trent and I will head to the grocery store and start cooking up meals to store in the freezer."

Stacia nodded and took a deep, but shaky, breath. "Sounds like we've got it all covered."

Trent looked out the window across the aisle from him. "I hope Abs still has the extra freezer.

"I'm almost sure she does." Raegan looked at her husband. "Last summer she said Jade and her friends would eat her out of house and home if she let them." She wiped a tear that started to fall and looked out her window. "I still can't believe it."

Trent ran his hand over his head. "I know. This is so crazy."

Quentin shook his head. "Man, it seems like just yesterday that Jade walked across the stage to get her diploma, and now..."

Stacia placed her hand over his. "I know."

"So, has anybody heard how Malcolm is handling this?" Raegan asked the question but was unsure if she wanted to hear the answer.

"Keith said he's doing all right, or as well as can be expected after watching your daughter die the same day you find out she exists." Trent acknowledged.

Stacia bowed her head slightly. "God help him."

Quentin put his arm around his wife. "God help them both. I can't imagine what Abril is going through right now."

***

Malcolm shut the door to Abril's room quietly and walked down the hallway. The doctor offered to write a prescription for something that would help her sleep while they were at the hospital, but she had declined it. She had been in a daze since she'd gotten those phone messages, earlier. He was in a daze as well. He continued walking until he reached the second bedroom of the townhome.

He flipped on the light and looked around. If he hadn't known better, it would have looked like any other generic combination of an office and guest room. But he did know better. This is where his daughter once slept, where she grew up. Abril had apparently cleared out any evidence of Jade's existence, on the surface anyway. He opened the closet door and found what he was looking for. A bulletin board filled with pictures.

He pulled it out, along with a small box tucked in the corner and sat down on the full-size bed. He studied the pictures on the board and smiled. She was full of life, and seemingly very popular. But then she would be, he thought, looking at her surrounded by friends. She was absolutely beautiful and, knowing Abril, she had a beautiful personality to match her outer beauty. He put the board aside and opened the box. He pulled out her yearbooks and class photos carefully, in order not to ruffle them.

He started with the most recent and worked his way back. She had random report cards and papers thrown in with pictures and small mementos. Everything he saw had an "A" or an "A+" on it. His eyes misted and he used the back of his hands to wipe them dry.

He went through everything in the box and read every word. He wanted to know the precious girl that had just slipped through his fingers. A box of stuff couldn't make up for the last twenty years, he knew, but it was a start. He held it together until he pulled out a picture of Jade in the first grade. Her front teeth were missing and she looked like an absolute angel. Malcolm stared at the photo and let the tears flow freely. He had missed all of it. He wept and shed tears for the girl he had never known and for the woman who would never get to see her dreams fulfilled.

He shook his head in sorrow. Was Abril so angry for twenty years that she kept this from him? What had he done to her that was so horrible that she wouldn't tell him about his own child? Okay, he would be the first person to admit that he had some issues in college, but who didn't? Everyone was young and stupid back then. Well, if she thought she was angry, she hadn't seen anything yet. He would give her time and let her grieve, but she had a lot to answer for. And she was going to hear everything he had to say about the matter.

After about an hour, he put the board and the box in the closet, and shut the door as his mind wandered back to the conversation with Morgana. She was sad and shocked, yes, but she wasn't surprised. He would bet that none of them would be surprised. His so-called best friends knew he had a child and never once bothered to mention it to him? Some friends. He now had to sit through a funeral for his own daughter that he barely knew, while they got to mourn and cherish their own memories of her. He was disgusted with the whole situation and didn't even want to see them when they showed up.

***

The next afternoon was a busy one. Garrison and Imani were the last couple to arrive at Abril's house. Quentin, Trent, and Keith walked out to help carry in the furniture they had picked up from the store earlier. Once that was done, everyone got back to work. They were all quietly milling about and going about their assigned tasks. They kept the noise level to a minimum, knowing Abril was trying to rest. Rumor had it that she nearly lost control when she saw the baby, who apparently looked just like Jade.

Malcolm descended the stairs slowly and looked at the group gathered around the house. He took a moment to glare at each person individually before he landed on the last step. They knew what the looks meant. He was silently asking each of them how they could call themselves his friend and not let him know that he had a child in college. He hadn't brought it up with Abril yet. She was in too much pain and there would be plenty of time for that later. He didn't say a word, but walked to the front of the house.

"How's Abril?" Keith asked the question right before Malcolm opened the front door.

"She's fine." And then he was gone.

"That went well." Imani went back to lining the bassinet.

"Cut him some slack. He's had a rough couple of days." Garrison looked over at his wife.

"I know." She looked sad. "I'm praying for him."

They put the baby's furniture together and cleared out the second bedroom. The guys moved Jade's bed to the basement and Abril's desk back to the living room. Stacia and the other ladies filled the closet and dresser with the new clothes and linen they'd purchased as the guys moved the furniture into the room. They transformed the former office and guestroom into a nursery fit for a princess. They were there until late that night working and had barely seen the grieving grandparents. Raegan made sure Abril got up and ate something before everyone left for the hotel.

***

Morgana finished brushing her teeth and grabbed the hairbrush from her overnight case. Keith went past her into the bathroom and she sat in front of the mirror in the bedroom. She was there only a moment before she heard a knock at the door. There was really only one hotel close to where Abril lived, and since it was nowhere near peak season, the place was practically empty. Everyone stayed at the same hotel so she assumed it was one of the girls coming to borrow something. She was completely surprised when she looked through the peephole and saw that it wasn't one of them.

"It's Malcolm."

"I'll be out in a sec." Keith called from the bathroom. She unlocked the door and then the chain lock that the hotel provided. She was completely unprepared when a drunk Malcolm, forcibly grabbed her and shoved her against the wall.

"Ouch!" Malcolm!"

"You knew!"

She tried to get away but he had a tight grip. "You've been drinking."

He laughed. "Have I? Oh, yeah, my so-called friends drove me to it. Isn't that something, five years sober, and all of it right down the toilet. But wait until you hear why. Do you know they actually hid the fact that I had a child from me for twenty years." He lifted her up and pushed her into the wall again. "You knew! For twenty years you knew that girl was alive and you never said anything."

Keith appeared out of nowhere and spoke a low warning into Malcolm's ear. "I don't want to kill you tonight, not after what you've been through, but I will. Put my wife down and step away from her."

Sensing that Keith was beyond serious, Malcolm lowered Morgana to the ground and took a step back. He quickly found himself against the wall with Keith's fist swiftly moving toward his face.

"Keith, don't!" Morgana screamed out. Keith just stopped himself and turned to look at her.

"Look at him. He's hurting."

The right reverend took a gulp of air and a step back. He looked his wife up and down. "Are you all right?"

She nodded quickly. "Yeah, I'm fine."

He saw that she was and kissed her hurriedly. "Baby, will you excuse us for awhile?"

"Yes, of course."

The two men started to walk out of the door, but Malcolm turned around.

"Morgana?"

"Yeah?"

"I'm sorry."

She eyed him for a moment before stepping forward. Morgana put her arms around him and waited. She could actually feel the turmoil swirling around inside of him, but she knew how most men held things in.

It only took a moment before he returned the embrace. Since he'd found out about Jade the night before, his life had literally been turned upside down. Abril was going through her own pain and couldn't comfort him. Yes, he was still angry with her and his friends but even in the haze of the liquor that filled his veins, he knew he needed this consoling. He held on to Morgana for dear life. It was a full minute before he let go.

"I'll be back soon," Keith kissed Morgana again and walked outside with Malcolm.

Whatever comfort Malcolm received from Morgana was short-lived. He lit into Keith when they hit the parking lot. He was so loud that Quentin, Garrison, and Trent couldn't help but hear him. They all got dressed quickly and joined the two men in the parking lot.

"Oh, now you come down? Where were you when I needed you? Where were you twenty years ago?"

"In the waiting room at Crawford-Long Hospital." Trent spoke calmly.

"What?" Malcolm looked over at him.

Quentin stared at Malcolm a moment before speaking. "That's where Jade was born, Crawford-Long, December 19, 1991."

"Oh, so this a joke?" Malcolm hollered again. "You think this is funny?"

Garrison shook his head. "No man, there's nothing funny about it. We were there and you weren't."

Malcolm's eyes looked liked they would pop out of his head. "You could have told me! That's not my fault!"

"Not your fault?" Keith's lips were drawn into one tight line. "Oh, you're right. What were we thinking? It's not your fault. You were held up that night. I believe it was the Schaffer sisters."

The alcohol binge that Malcolm participated in earlier was starting to affect him. He looked as if he could fall out at any minute. "What the hell are you talking about?"

"That night, you screwed the Schafer twins. You were excited because it was your first threesome." Keith reminded him.

Trent nodded. "Yeah, all of us asked you that night if you wanted to hang out. We were going to tell you."

Quentin placed his finger on the side of his face. "Right, but if I remember correctly, your exact words were, "There couldn't possibly be anything in the world more important tonight than doing two girls at the same time."

Malcolm leaned back against his rental car. "I said that?"

Trent nodded again. "Yeah, you did."

"But wait, there's more!" Garrison said it in his T.V. announcer voice and evoked a smile out of everyone but Malcolm. "What do you remember about the night you and Abril broke up?"

Malcolm tried to remember that night, but couldn't.

When he didn't answer, Keith nodded. "Yeah, that makes sense. You were piss-drunk and in bed with some girl you picked up at the club that night."

Malcolm shook his head. "I don't recall that."

Keith was exasperated. "I don't recall that? This is not a congressional hearing Malcolm, this is your life we're talking about, here!"

Malcolm simply shrugged. "I don't remember."

"Oh, okay. Let me see if I can help you." Keith pushed himself off the car and walked toward Malcolm. "Abril showed up at the door crying and freaking out because she'd just found out that she was pregnant. She banged on the door and when you opened it and she saw the naked girl in your bed, that only caused her to freak out more."

Malcolm grabbed his head. Scenes from the distant past started to invade his head, but he wasn't sure what he was seeing. "I don't..."

"Yeah, you do." Keith egged him on. "Think about it. The girl had hooters the size of Texas. I still remember that."

"I don't remember. I mean…"

"You stepped out the room with this stupid grin on your face and put on quite a show. Everybody came out of their dorm rooms to watch."

Malcolm continued to shake his head.

"You cursed her out until she broke down in tears and ran away. You called her everything but a child of God, and then you told her not to bother you again."

Malcolm slumped against the car. "And she didn't."

Quentin placed a hand on Malcolm's shoulder. "No, she didn't. And we couldn't blame her. When Jade got a little older, you still hadn't changed and Abril wasn't trying to deal with your mess. She said she wouldn't put Jade in danger with an alcoholic father. She made us swear not to say anything."

Malcolm nodded with understanding. "And you all kept quiet."

"We were happy to, especially after you burned down that wing of your house." Trent's eyes told the whole story. "We all loved that little girl and we swore to protect her."

"Even from her own father, if we had to." Garrison agreed.

Malcolm put both hands on either side of his head to stop the pounding. "I had no idea. I mean I woke up and didn't remember anything. I called her once or twice but she never returned my calls."

Trent looked over at Malcolm. "To be honest with you, I'm surprised you saw Jade before she passed."

Malcolm looked up at the stars. "I think that was divine intervention."

Keith smiled. "Amen. Look, Mal, you've wasted a lot of time the last twenty years and you missed a lot. Jade was a great kid. If you were smart you'd stop wasting time here and go find out how special your daughter was."

Malcolm stood up slowly. He pulled his car keys out of his pocket and looked at his friends with watery eyes and slurred speech. "You know what, you're right. I think I'll do that."

Garrison held his hand out. "Hey, give me the keys."

"What?"

"You're drunk, and friends don't let friends drive drunk. Give me the keys."

Malcolm started to laugh but it turned into sobs quickly. Keith put his arm around the grieving father and let him cry.

"She called me daddy twice. Twice, then she died."

The men comforted their friend until he was ready for Garrison to drive him back over to Abril's house. Garrison took him to an all-night coffee shop first to sober him up. The sun was just coming up as he climbed out of the car and walked up to the house. Malcolm pulled out the key Abril had given him earlier and inserted it. The door was shut quickly and he tried to be quiet, in order not to disturb Abril. He closed and locked the door behind

152

him, only to find Abril sitting on the sofa and staring out the front window.

He noticed dry tear stains on her face and walked over to where she was sitting. He sat down beside her and took her hand. "Hi."

"Hi." She spoke in a whisper.

"I want you to tell me about Jade, everything you can remember, but first I need to apologize for the last twenty years."

She used the balled up tissue in her hand to dry her damp eyes. "Those are over and done with, you don't need to apologize for that, Malcolm."

He slid off the couch and knelt in front of her. "Yes, I do. I was self absorbed and only interested in satisfying myself. I neglected and abused you and the gift you gave me and I know there are no words to make up for what I did, but if you'll let me, I will spend the next forty years making them up to you. Please let me."

Abril began to cry again. "I don't even know how to get past tomorrow, much less the next forty years."

He pushed himself up off the floor and sat down next to her again. He hugged her tightly and let her cry until she became silent. When the tears subsided, he tilted her face up so that they were looking in each other's eyes. "Can we try together? There's a beautiful and nearly healthy baby girl lying in the hospital waiting for us to come get her. We would be doing the baby and her mother a disservice if that child receives anything less than our best. Now, tell me about Jade."

She knew what he was doing. He was trying to get her mind off the death of their daughter and on to the life of their new granddaughter. The only problem was, she didn't know if she could do it again. Jade had taken her heart with her when she slipped away the other night. Abril didn't know how she was going to do it again.

"It's all right if you don't feel it right now." He must have guessed what she was thinking. He pulled her closer and whispered in he ear. "I'll carry you for as long as you need me to." She cried again. When she stopped this time, she dried her tears and picked up a large scrapbook off the floor and opened it.

She stared down at the book, but didn't move. "Thank you, Malcolm."

He kissed her temple slowly and let his lips linger there. "It's my pleasure. Now, tell me about our daughter. "

Abril inhaled deeply and nodded. "Well, she is... was, she was extremely stubborn."

He nodded. "Mmm, she probably got that from my Granny."

He said it without a hint of amusement in his voice, but Abril laughed at him anyway. "Granny's not the only one with a stubborn streak."

He smiled. "No, I guess not. How did she handle money? She took after her old man didn't she? I bet she was a saver."

Abril dried her wet face for the umpteenth time that weekend and laughed again. "She spent every cent that came through her hands. She didn't know the meaning of the word 'save'. She probably would have drained your accounts dry."

154

A wistful smile lit his face. "She sounds perfect. What else?"

Abril smiled. "She was ridiculously smart. She tested in the top two percent of her class since kindergarten."

He smiled again. "That's my girl. I wish I could have talked to her. I wonder if she kept any journals?"

Abril nodded. "She did. I just found them this morning." She took a deep breath and thought about her angel. Yes, it was hard talking about her, now that she was gone, but it was doing her heart some good. She felt like she was getting the chance to brag on her baby one more time. "And she was very artistic. I have some of her artwork upstairs if you want to see it."

"I would love to."

***

Stacia smiled warmly while she packed her suitcase. Quentin walked into the hotel room and saw her.

"What's that goofy look for?"

She threw a luggage tag at him and laughed. "I was not looking goofy. I was just thinking about Malcolm and Abril. He's handling all of this really well. I don't know what you guys said to him that night, but it worked."

Quentin came in and wrapped his arms around her. "Let's just say we helped him see the error of his ways."

She looked up and smiled at her fiancé. "I'm proud of him, proud of all of you, actually. You all really stepped up when Abby needed it."

He shrugged. "We're her friends, too. We just did what friends naturally do. We help each other when we need it."

She laid her head on his chest and inhaled deeply. "You know, I don't know why it took all of this to make me see what's important. Our wedding was getting to be more about the crowd than us. I think I'll go reevaluate that guest list when we get home. "

He bent down and kissed her lips. "Yeah, this weekend opened my eyes to a lot of things too. You can invite as many people to our wedding as you want. All of a sudden, proving a point doesn't seem so important."

"I know." Stacia squeezed him tighter. "I still can't believe she's gone. She texted me last month to ask if she could come visit."

He nodded. "She did the same thing with me. She was probably trying to make arrangements in case Abril blew her cool."

"Yeah, and it was understandable. I know Abby would have been furious with her if she'd…"

"If she'd lived. You're right, but I also know Abril would give anything to have her back right now."

"Yeah. I think that little Jada Marie is going to be more of a blessing than anyone could have guessed."

Quentin agreed. "I know Malcolm thinks so. He's looking at this like a second chance. But hurry and finish packing please. We want to leave enough time to say our goodbyes."

She took one last look around the room. "I'm ready."

***

Abril hugged her friends one more time. She wouldn't have been able to make it through this nightmare without them. They had taken care of everything. Her freezer was packed with enough food to feed an army for several months. And Jada's new nursery was stocked to the brim with everything the baby would ever need for the next few years of life. She looked around at them and a fresh collection of tears welled up. It seemed she had a never-ending supply nowadays.

"You guys have a safe trip back."

Stacia hugged Abril around the neck. "We will. I want pictures every week, and you better call if you need anything."

Quentin laughed before hugging Malcolm and Abril. "I think Malcolm's got it covered, baby. Look at him. The baby's not even two weeks old and she's got Malcolm wrapped around her little finger."

"Does it show?" Malcolm almost looked worried. The room was filled with laughter moments later.

"Yeah, man." Garrison hugged Abril and then Malcolm. "It shows."

"It definitely shows." Imani hugged the happy couple next. "But that's all right. You have our permission to spoil her to pieces."

Malcolm smiled down at the beautiful little girl sleeping in his arms. "I think I'll take you up on that. She's going to be spoiled rotten."

Abril shook her head with the wisdom of someone who had raised a child. "No she's not."

Raegan reached in and hugged all three of them after Trent finished. "Go easy on him, Abs. You know how first time fathers are."

Trent looked at the happy family. "Aw, he'll be fine. You two take care."

Morgana and Keith brought up the rear.

"I want pictures every week, too... unless, you're moving to Atlanta soon? Then I can come take them myself."

Abril glanced at Malcolm out the corner of her eye. "Well, now that you mention it..."

Malcolm adjusted the baby before looking up. "Yes, they will definitely be joining me down in Atlanta."

The room was suddenly filled with cheers and high-fives. Malcolm instinctively covered the baby's ears. "Hey, what are you all trying to do, kill her hearing? Get out of here with that noise."

Keith just shook his head. He hugged Malcolm and Abril, then turned around to the rest of the group. "Come on, guys let's get out of here. We've got papa bear riled up."

Malcolm tapped his chest. "That's right and don't you forget who runs this house."

Imani looked over her shoulder on her way out the door. "Um, we know who runs the house."

"Sure do." Stacia nodded.

"Without a doubt." Morgana agreed.

"Mama bear runs this house." Abril said with finality.

Raegan added an extra "mmmhmm," for good measure before everyone filed out of the house.

Epilogue

More than three hundred guests sat on the expanse of land that was Malcolm's back yard and waited for the ceremony to begin. The bridal party began to line up behind the white folding chairs. The groomsmen stood waiting near the podium, looking handsome in their tuxedos. The music started and everyone was set to begin, everyone except the flower girl.

"Mommy!" The little girl whispered in a panic.

Morgana bent down and looked at her daughter. "What is it, baby?"

"I don't want to go down by myself."

"It's okay, honey. Just do it like we practiced, remember? Just drop some flower petals on the white paper then go stand near your uncles and wait for me and your aunties."

"No." Little Ashlyn shook her head with determination.

Morgana sighed and looked around until she spotted her son. "Mark, walk with your sister then come back and stand with the rest of the junior ushers, please."

"Okay, mom."

Morgana smiled when, after making sure his sister was all right, Mark and Keith did a fist bump.

Imani spotted her triplets sitting with the Nanny and blew kisses to them. She turned and gave a wink to Garrison, who was standing with the rest of the men. When the wedding coordinator gave the signal,

Morgana, Imani and Raegan strolled down the aisle followed by a very pregnant Stacia. Quentin smiled at his wife, praying the baby wouldn't make an early appearance, for all their sakes.

All the ladies stood where they were supposed to and turned expectantly. The large crowd stood and prepared to receive the bride. Abril made the most beautiful vision in white. She was glowing and gliding. She walked the length of the aisle and went to stand next to Malcolm. She handed her bouquet to Morgana and flashed Malcolm a smile.

Reverend Belton cleared his throat and began, "Dearly beloved, we are gathered here today, in the sight of God and..." He tried but couldn't continue because one particular baby was making an obscene amount of noise.

"Mama! Mama! Mama!"

Abril gathered the front of her dress and walked down the three stairs of the podium. She scooped Jada from Granny's lap and hurried back to the small stage.

She kissed the baby and smiled bashfully. "Sorry about that. We can continue now."

The older man smiled patiently and began again. "Dearly beloved, we are gathered here today, in the sight of God and this great crowd, to witness the joining of Abril Elaine Barnes and Malcolm Calder in holy matrimony..."

END

Dear Readers,

I hope you enjoyed The Re-Mix. I've already cast the movie version in my mind. I would love to hear from readers who you think should play each character. If you'd like to read more stories like this one, please contact me and let me know which characters you'd like to hear more about. You can contact me on Facebook and leave a comment about the book. If you enjoyed this book, please consider leaving a review on the site where the book was purchased.

Thanks so much for your support!

Xandra

Peace and Blessings